The
Wisdom
Seeker

The Wisdom Seeker

William E. Dickinson

This is a work of fiction. Names, characters, places and incidents either are the product
of the author's imagination or are used fictitiously, and any resemblance to any actual
persons, living or dead, events, or locales is entirely coincidental.

This book was printed in the United States of America.

To order additional copies of this book, contact:
Xlibris Corporation
1-888-795-4274
www.Xlibris.com
Orders@Xlibris.com
40636

Index

Thanks to Edwin Redman without whom
this novel would have been impossible.

Past Still Mean

@#$%@#$%@#$%@#$%@#$%

A man from violent past
His heritage through karma seen
Seeking only peace and knowledge
His path, not vision mean

Yet, the wisdom of the ages
Seen through martial skills
Substantial and insubstantial
A place in life to fill

While rooted in the past
With solid hand blade clean
The "Wisdom Seeker" may find that place
But, the past can still be seen

William E.Dickinson
Author and Poet

Chapter 1

The Wisdom Seeker

As Mark Trembley entered the university campus, peace of mind began to invade his tortured soul. His quick easy stride, and easy grin covered a slight uneasiness at being a post Vietnam Student. This meticulously attired man had a meeting with the head of the Humanities Department, Dean Anders. But, fate was to delay this meeting!

Mark suddenly realized that he had left his discharge papers in his car! He turned, and retraced his steps, to the amusement of a group of students who were watching with interest.

Josh Logan, Football Captain, man about town, and recruiter, noted with interest Mark's quick and powerful strides.

As Mark crossed the wide and busy street, he noticed a child in the middle of the road.

Mark looked quickly to the right, and to the left. An eighteen wheeler coming around the corner was bearing down on the child. To his right, at about two hundred yards was a station wagon with the back "door" open. It had just come to an abrupt stop! Dropping his open briefcase, Marc sprinted with powerful strides between the parked cars to the child. While still on the run he stooped down and scooped the child into his arms. He reached the other side of the road just as the truck came to a screeching halt, fifty feet beyond Mark and the frightened child! Mark had dived and tumbled the last few feet to safety!

The little five year old was scared, but otherwise unharmed, except for abrasions and some cuts. Mark Trembley on the other hand was a complete mess! His new sport *coat from Jordan's was cut under the arms, and smeared with the child's blood. His tie was more grease than green. Mark's brown slacks were rumpled and dirty, but not torn.*

Mark was only slightly dazed, so he sat up, to the absolute delight of the gathering crowd.

Suddenly Mark was lifted to his feet. The strong arms of a very happy truck driver encircled Mark's body like a powerful chain. The big red faced man had lifted Mark to his feet and now shook his hand, even as tears streamed down his cheeks.

Mark consoled the man to the delight of the enlarged crowd.

Suddenly, to Mark's complete surprise a kiss was placed on his cheek!

Showing an embarrassed smile Mark let go of the truckdriver's pumping hand to confront the bestower of the kiss! A young moist-eyed redhead stood beaming before him! Judith McPhearson was filled with gratitude for this man who had just saved her Allison from harm.

She suddenly placed her supple body against his in instant gratitude! Mark's taunt body returned the favor, with utter delight!

Mark suddenly remembered the interview with Dean Anders! He blurted out a "Good by. I must be going" as he left the confused scene! Mark now sprinted to his Carrera, which was parked nearby.

He collected all the papers from his car, and then retrieving those that he had dropped he again sprinted towards the Dean's office. Josh Logan and his friends applauded as he passed by them.

"I know a good runner when I see one," exclaimed Josh! "I'll recruit him, or my name ain't Josh Logan!"

"Sure Josh, and were all going to be millionaires" chided his teammates in unison! Josh's face got red as a beet.

As Mark rushed towards the administration building he felt good about his present actions, damn good! But, he thought it best not tell of his clandestine past in Special Forces and CIA. He would have to tell the Dean a little more than name, rank and serial number.

What would the Dean of Humanities think of a professional trained to kill in dozens of ways, armed or unarmed? His athletic six foot frame had been tuned to the utmost, and he had used it to complete many deadly tasks. In war it had seemed justified, but as a civilian agent it had finally got to him and he quit.

Integral to Captain Mark Trembley's tough military training was comradeship. In his anxiety this was easier to tackle than Agent 321 as a cold calculating killer. The cold, the mud, the sharp steel, but still it was a team! This team trained and finally tuned for a mission. The mission seemed to have a goal beyond itself. Was this patriotism, accomplishment, or what else? Mark had enjoyed the tough training, and "yes" the danger set his adrenaline soaring! But, alone as an instrument of death seeking out his unsuspecting quarry brought home the stark reality of mortality! The "Wisdom Seeker" was evolving. At first the killing was a thrill, but it was coupled with patriotism. This was the essential element that was missing, and it was too personal. As an agent it was too mechanical. Just too cut and dry! In a military situation there was always ameliorating circumstances.

Dean Anders looked up from his papers as the Vietnam Veteran Mr. Mark Trembley entered his office. Trembley was about six feet tall with blonde hair. He was good looking in a rugged kind of way. He looked solid and athletic, but he was not tidy. His clothes were soiled and creased, and he was sweating. What had happened to him?

"You are one half hour late Mr. Trembley. Please have a seat," Anders instructed Mark.

Dean Anders was a "high brow" of the first order, but a just man.

"So. You are interested in the humanities," the dean said to the disheveled man seated before him. Anders followed the critical observations with a series of general questions. He was pleasantly surprised with the quick, concise and accurate answers from Mark.

The answer he gave for his unfortunate appearance, was that he had an accident. This was his only hesitation in an otherwise flawless response to Anders questions.

Yet the clandestine nature of the CIA and Special Forces and Trembley's employ by them made Anders a bit uneasy. Former Captain Mark R. Trembley seemed ready for university, but was university ready for him?

Chapter 2

The Boarding House

Mark's Masters Degree program was all set. He also registered for an additional literature class, that met twice a week.

He decided to live off campus, thinking it would be quieter. The boarding house he found was about a mile from the campus. It was located in a neighborhood of mixed Black, White and Hispanic Races. Mrs. Vincinto, the owner showed him to his room. When she left he was glad to be alone in this clean spare room. It had a big old double bed, two chairs, a dresser, an overstuffed chair and a table in it. Unfortunately the only shower was two doors down at the end of the hall!

As cleanliness is close to Godliness, he thought a shower is the best that he could do for the moment! On the way to the shower a man bumped into him, and with an apalogetic grunt continued on his way. The man was young and rather dirty(having come from the direction of the shower)! Mark instinctively reached for his wallet, but it was gone! He turned quickly and saw the man who had bumped into him hurriedly heading for the stairs to the street. Mark sprinted toward the man. He caught the man just as he reached the street door at the foot of the stairs.

Mark's right arm came up and down in a quick karate chop to the neck of the fleeing man. The young thief went sprawling through the street door and landed in a crumpled heap on the front stairs. A thin trickle of blood dripped from his mouth onto the white marble stair and onto the sidewalk.

A small group of angry neighbors and passers-by immediately gathered to see who had hurt this young man!

Mark tried to explain that the man was a thief, but to no avail!

In a few minutes the police arrived.

"What Is going on here? Who hurt this boy?" A burly policeman asked of the crowd! A couple who had witnessed the episode finally spoke up.

"This guy went after the boy and struck him down" they exclaimed!

"Search the boy and you will find my wallet"

Mark suggested. When they did this he was able to convince them that he was the victim and not the perpetrator of this situation!

Mark chuckled to himself when he realized why he was unable to convince the police of his innocence! His attire consisted of a pair of slacks, and nothing else.

Mark gave Police Corporal Crowley a statement explaining the theft in detail. They were surprised that he was able to chase this young boy down a flight of stairs and catch him at the front door, particularly when they checked the police log and found his moniker to be "Fleet Foot". It turned out the boy had a record of thefts, and probations. It also turned out he was called "Fleet Foot" by the officers who tried to catch him, for he usually got away!

"That was pretty extreme for a petty theft", said Crowley to Mark. "You're a rather violent man Mr. Trembley".

With this skepticism Crowley dismissed Mark.

"Thank you" said Mark. He then returned to the boarding house.

He was greeted by the landlady, Mrs. Vincento. She warned him about being rowdy and fighting on her premises. He tried to explain, but to no avail.

Mark returned to the bathroom to get his much needed shower. After a hot shower he returned to his spare room for some Tai Chi, Chi Kung and meditation. Relaxed now, he wondered if his vivid memory would recall all the old subjects again? Tomorrow he would find out, it was his first day of his Masters in Humanities Program!

Chapter 3

The First Day

Mark was a sight to behold(this 35 year old post Vietnam Student) in a sea of jeans and scraggy hair! His rugged six foot frame, with blonde hair and deep blue eyes, and cat-like walk made him stand out.

Marc wore a light gray shirt with a pale blue tie, dark gray slacks and a navy blue blazer. His attire ended with grey loafers. His new image was topped off with a thin leather briefcase.

This emergence into a highly visible academic profile was ironic not withstanding his clandestine background in Special Forces and as an undercover agent. But this would be a very satisfying change, quite relaxing.

Personal remarks from some of the men, and a few cheers from a few women made it a little comical. Marc ignored them all with a little shrug of the shoulders.

This first class(Ancient History), was an elective that should be a breeze because of his long background in foreign cultures. In his 15 years in government employment Marc had come to love the brutalized and hard working peasants of the world. He did not have the same love for their governments! He had been trained in the cultures of many Asian, South and Central American countries. He had seen their struggle to survive.

The entrance of this older student was noted with interest by the professor. Professor McNamara was pleased to have a handsome, and mature man in her class. He would probably do well in her class.

The second class, Conversational Spanish, was also to his liking. Marc's ace in this class was his military prep course in Spanish, and the use of the language in his many sojourns into South and Central America for Special Forces, and others.

Mr. Rojas, the Spanish Professor, by class end took an irrational dislike to this too quick witted older student!

As Marc was leaving the Spanish Class he was approached by a big burly red headed man.

"Hello, I'm Josh Logan the unofficial recruiter for the football team"! I watched you rescue that child in the road. It showed good power and particularly speed. We need some of both on our losing team, were desperate! Could you come to a practice and "try-out"?

Logan held his hand out, and Marc responded in a firm clasp.

Not being the soul of tact, Logan launched into another pitch on the needs of the football team. "When I saw that display of yours saving that child, I thought that was a good end run if ever I saw one! Join our team, we badly need a good strong end."

"Damn it this guy will play football or else," thought Logan! His temper was rising and his face was red.

"I'm sorry football isn't my sport anymore", Marc answered. He started to leave the classroom. To Marc's surprise, he was grabbed by Logan and thrust against the wall! Instinctively Marc's knee came up in a powerful thrust into Logan's groin. Logan loosened his grip as the pain crept into his brain. In a blur of motion Marc's hand came up in a Chin Na Hammer Hand move, but he relaxed as Logan was "neutralized" and unable to respond because of the pain. The big fullback collapsed against Professor Rojas's desk in a heap!

Marc was exasperated that he had to use force on this unfortunate hulk of a man, but pleased his composure returned.

Professor Rojas was both scared and furious with this disturbing incident! He wanted to expel Marc. Several students confirmed Marc's story that he was grabbed and thrust against the wall.

For the first time Rojas spoke to this new violent student. "Mr. Trembley, you had better explain all this to the Dean of Students".

While Rojas was talking, Logan recovered and hurriedly left the room.

Marc apologized to Professor Rojas, and left for Dean Anders office for a review and explanation of the incident.

Dean Anders was disturbed and puzzled by the call he had just received from Professor Rojas. What was a Dean to do with a man who rescues a child one day and destroys athletes the very next day? The Dean was still pondering this same question when Marc was ushered into his office.

Marc entered Anders office, and once again knew he would look like a brawling bum. With this in mind he faced this distinguished gentleman seated behind his large oak desk.

"Please sit down Mr. Trembley", Dean Anders directed.

"Does the university experience seem too tame for you Mr. Trembley? Or, are you unable to leave your past behind? Please explain what happened Mr. Trembley. I'm all ears."

Marc described the incident in graphic detail. The Dean listened to the entire episode in silence, then he began to castigate Marc.

This castigation did not come directly, but in veiled sociological references. A lecture followed on "Humanism and Order". This could have come directly from the Intelligence Community, but hardly from the Dean of Students at a university!

The former Captain Marc Trembley's mind drifted back to many lectures on the very same subject.

Marc was brought back to the present with a stern warning. "You must avoid trouble at all costs" was Anders very pointed advice! He continued "The first cost to you would be expulsion. The next would be the police."

"Are your hands registered as "lethal weapons" with the police?"

A surprised answer of "no", came from Marc! Marc explained, "I can not even register in the private sector for two years! I can not do this as a matter of security".

Do you understand Mr. Anders?

"No, but I will find out", came Anders reply.

The Dean now continued his admonishment. It is therefore agreed that you will avoid all hint of trouble while at this university?

"Yes," said Marc, with obvious relief.

To seal the bargain they clasped hands. Marc was surprised by the steel like grip of this academic!

When Marc left the Dean he had the distinct impression that there was more to the man below the surface then appeared.

The rest of the day was uneventful, with only a course in Sociology to complete the day's study.

Marc left the campus. He picked up some wine, cheese, and crackers before returning to his kitchen and bedroom apartment(such as it was).

Marc glanced out of the window before turning in for the night. On the street he noticed a black Camero Z28 not a Formula Trans-Am(like yesterday). The cars engine was running as it was parked amidst the Beetles and Datsuns across the street.

Chapter 4

A New Man

Tuesday was the second day of classes, Marc was about to "ascend" to the campus stage! This "new man" wore three ply denim jeans, heavy black belt, white T-shirt with pocket, and suede sneakers.

The theory was, if you see trouble you will avoid it! Marc Trembley looked like trouble with his leather wrist bands covering powerful wrists, with powerful arms and shoulders to match. Dog tags on a gold chain encircled his strong neck. Marc was now mean to be seen! To complete the impression a green beret was folded neatly in his belt.

Marc's first class was conducted by none other than Dean Anders who was substituting for the regular professor.

The Dean was amused by the new Marc Trembley before him, but not surprised.

A cautious man once wrote "To know is good, but to know first is better." This crossed Anders mind at the sight of the new Marc Trembley.

Anders had checked Marc's references, but did not get all the facts he would have liked. With a little help from a military friend the Dean did get some basic information on Captain Marc R. Trembley. They did confirm that he was a Captain in Special Forces. He was a "specialist". The friend could not find out what kind of specialist. When he asked if Trembley had any "Degrees", the answer was, "4 degrees listed", Sir! Subsequently it was found out that they were a B. A. in

The Humanities, and 3 degrees in Martial Arts(unspecified). The Administrative Specialist had candidly voiced Dean Anders own present thoughts. "Definitely a man to avoid," Sir! The CIA on the other hand would not even confirm that Captain Marc R. Trembley even existed! But, they protested a bit too much for Anders friend to take their word. After several referrals a Mr. Alton would only confirm Marc R. Trembley's starting date with the agency.

Regional Manager Latin America Fredric Alton laid down the "cleared" phone with satisfaction He now had absolute confirmation of his dissident agent Marc Trembley's whereabouts. That sob. who blew it by killing his contact for all of Central America would pay dearly for that damned conscience of his!

The Deans mind drifted back to his substitute Sociology Class.

Anders first question was to Mr. Marc Trembley.

"Mr. Trembley, is man a social animal?"

"Yes", was Marc's reply. "But, other animals are social as well."

This did not stop the questioning.

Dean Anders continued, "Then why is it that man alone fights for personal advantage?" Marc's answer was, "man can be flawed in the use of his higher intelligence."

"Flawed in what way Mr. Trembley?"

"There is an inherent arrogance in knowing right from wrong", Marc said.

"Doesn't that mean that animals are immoral?," the Dean continued.

The questions began to bother Marc, and to hang heavy on his mind. He began to sweat.

"No!" Came his answer, "because this is a human trait and condition."

"Then are animals better than humans?" asked the Dean.

Not waiting for a reply the Dean thanked the prisoner of the moment, as if he was pardoned!

Marc smiled, and thought, "there is one person I haven't fooled!"

Marc's next lecture was not for an hour, so he sauntered over to the cafeteria for a much needed coffee. He looked over his steaming cup of coffee to see the battered face of Josh Logan sitting at the end of the counter with two burly friends. It was obvious from the pained expression on Logan's face that he had not forgotten their confrontation! Neither party acknowledged the other.

Marc decided to get the cafeterias "special", take his last class, and then return to the boarding house.

When he returned to his apartment at the boarding house he picked up his books for his night course in English. As he bent over the bureau(he used for a desk), he saw a black Trans-Am parked across the street. Looking closely he saw two men in business suits sitting in the front seat. A third man was sitting in the shadows of the back seat. This was the second or third time he had seen a black Trans-Am or Camero Z28 parked very close to the boarding house, and with the motor running! Should he be careful? If so, of what?

Chapter 5

Night Class

Marc was a meticulous man so he decided that the "tough guy look" was not necessary for the expected older night class students. A sport shirt, dockers, suede shoes, and golfing jacket would do nicely.

When he arrived for the English Class he was surprised to still find the casual wear he had found on days. It was no wonder people looked around when he entered, late!

Mrs. Sullivan, a pretty, thin, and earnest blonde of about thirty asked if he was the late registered student, Marc Trembley?

His yes satisfied her query, and he sat down.

Mrs. Sullivan was a divorcee, and thought it was going to be nice to have an attractive man in her class!

Marc had taken a seat at the rear of the raised classroom so that he could see the rest of the class. From his point of good visibility he could see that a redhead in the front row was being "bothered" by a youth to her right. He kept trying to put his arm around her shoulder or lean against her so that she couldn't even write on her clipboard! Most of this went unnoticed by Mrs. Sullivan. Even though it met with little success, it was still annoying to the woman.

The red headed woman seemed vaguely familiar, even from the back of the classroom.

At the class break, the rows behind her cleared so that Marc wondered down to the row behind, to see if he knew her. As he sat down he saw the woman was the mother of the little girl in the street.

Marc said hello, "May I be of assistance?" Even as he spoke he placed a vice like grip on the muscles of the annoying boy's neck with his right hand!

The woman smiled, and turned to greet Marc with a nervous, "Hello!"

The youth on the other hand was hurting. His face was turning ashen, and then to white as Marc released his grip.

The youth got up and stumbled out of the room without a word. Only a groan of pain was heard.

Marc moved to the front row, and confirmed that it was indeed Allicin's mother he had rescued this time!

"Are you okay" Marc inquired?

"It was annoying and embarrassing, "answered the lady.

Judith McPherson introduced herself. In the subsequent conversation it turned out that she was a divorcee(in her mid thirties) trying to improve her skills, and life-style

"Yes, and it's thanks again to . . .", she asked!

"It's Marc, Marc Trembley at your service!"

"How is little Allicin?", Marc inquired.

"She's fine, maybe you could come and see her sometime."
"I'd like that," Marc responded. Marc's interest in the college scene visibly increased.
"It would have to be on a weekend because of school, days for Allicin and nights for me," she explained.

"That would be fine," responded Marc.

"Do you have a job at the university," Marc asked?

Marc's pleasant demeanor allowed Judy to vent a little frustration. No I don't. This was a sour chapter in Judy's life. She explained that she had a part time job but couldn't get full time employment because of Allicin's school days. Her night courses cost her dearly for a baby sitter. She did have a small alimony settlement, but no help from the, government at all.

When Marc asked, Judy agreed to meet Marc for a coffee after class. It would have to be short as the baby sitter was expensive.

A beautiful spring evening greeted Marc and Judy as they walked to a nearby coffee shop. Marc's whole body relaxed as he guided Judy down the stairs between students. They sat down at a table at Raffiel's Coffee Bar, just a block from the university.

Judy McPherson only talked in generalities at the coffee shop. She did ask Marc what he did for a living.

"I worked for the government after I left the Army," he responded.

"What did you do in the Army," she continued?

"I was a Captain in Special Forces, but I can't say more than that, ", was his reluctant response.

"Sounds mysterious" she replied.

"No, just dirty like all army jobs" he conceded.

Marc was intrigued by this beautiful woman, and comfortable about his friendship with this personable, Judith McPherson.

Judy now excused herself in order to get back at a reasonable time.

Marc walked Judy back to the parking lot, and managed to get a date in two weeks time. As he was walking her to the car he had a foreboding presentiment of being watched. He reminded himself that he was a civilian now, and just being paranoid.

For the next two weeks Marc was occupied with class work, and homework. University life was beginning to numb his senses to any impending doom, or potential hazard.

On the second weekend following the semester's start Marc had his second date with Judy. It was a beautiful evening, but it had a slight nip in the air. Marc's 944 pulled smoothly into a parking spot near Judy's house. As Marc got out of the car he noticed a black Trans-Am parked across the street. He was vaguely curious, but dismissed the car without a second glance as he went to Judy's front steps.

Marc's skin began to crawl as he saw the door was ajar, and the curtains were all drawn. His field training as an agent began to take over. Too many coincidences; The black Trans-Am. The feeling of being watched. And, now a door ajar and the curtains down when Judy was expecting him! Marc now carefully checked the outside of the house. He saw no sign of forced entry. Approaching the front door with catlike grace, he heard someone crying in the front room. Judy was in the center of the room sitting on a pile of debris, crying. Her hair was disheveled, her face bruised and bleeding. Her blouse was torn half off her shoulders. Her jeans were torn, and the belt was missing.

Marc could feel the anger, and the tenderness welling up within his body. The room looked Like a tornado had hit it. His eyes came back to the plight of the figure before him.

"My God, Judy, what happened?" Marc asked gently.

He put his arm around Judy's shoulder, and tried to comfort her. Then the story began to unfold.

'Three men came to the door, and when I answered they forced their way into the house," Judy blurted out! She continued "They had masks on and they grabbed me, Marc!"

"I was so scared that I couldn't talk or yell! The biggest one with the red hair beat and assaulted me" Judy cried!

"Did they say anything about why they were doing this," Marc inquired?

*"They did say that my friend had better play along and be more cooperative,"
was Judy's recollection as she began to gain her composure.*

*Would even a screwed up football player go this far to force him to play
football Marc thought to himself? He had seen enough screwed up people not to
discount it either. But who else would do this? Who, but Logan had anything to
gain from this sorry episode? His answer to himself, was no one. The message was
clear, "Play football, or else!" A clear and chilling voice seemed to emanate from
deep within Marc, "Sure, I'll play football."*

*Judy can't stay here Marc thought. Until she is safe I can't do anything about
Mr. Logan.*

*Judy's composure was beginning to return, and with it's return her disheveled
appearance became an irritant to her. She excused herself.*

"I'm a mess, a real mess" Judy exclaimed!

"Sure Judy," Marc responded softly. I'll tidy up a bit.

Judy just nodded, and left the room.

*The room was also a mess. chairs were broken, a table knocked over, cushions
from the sofa where strewn around the room and a stand-up light was smashed.
But, on second look it wasn't as bad as it first looked.*

*Was this just a warning? A cruel episode for Judy. The assault on Judy was
a very different thing. It couldn't be tolerated. It really made his blood boil. This
would have to be dealt with!*

*When Judy returned, all clean and tidy Marc realized for the first time just
how beautiful she was. She was also vulnerable.*

*Across town Dale McAdams was discussing his new mission with fellow
conspirators John Anders and Ralph Johnson. "This" should be easier than those
Special Forces Tactical missions in the Golden Triangle! Although this Trembley
was a tough babe, we softened him up with the use of second parties to rough up
his girl friend. The guys were ringers for us!"*

"Yeah", said Anders, "these tough guys with a conscience always cave in when a friend is threatened!"

Johnson just nodded in agreement.

Anders recollected a story he heard about Trembley which alluded to the fact that Trembley had the "Death Touch!" "The story was that Trembley didn't use it unless he was in a combat situation, or he "lost it!" "When they lost it they were at a disadvantage", exclaimed Anders!

Ralph Johnson was not so certain, if memory served him correctly, he remembered two things that were disturbing: One was that Captain Marc Trembley had been dubbed "The Wisdom Seeker!" Two was that he had been present when Trembley had reacted like greased lightning in a training session(to save a sergeant from getting stabbed)! It was instinctive, fast, and could have been deadly. A fraction of an inch more and the well trained corporal would have been dead. Except when he was on a tactical mission, he always did the good thing.

"I can't leave you here, Judy. It just isn't safe" Marc insisted!

"What is the alternative" Judy asked?

"I can get you a room at my boarding house. It would be safer and I could look after you."

"I feel responsible, it's just because you know me that this happened" he explained.

"Could Allicin stay with a relative until we find out what is going on?". This was Marc's second proposal.

Judy was glad that Marc had suggested alternatives, because with all her bravado, she was still very soared! She just knew that Marc could be depended upon. Who else could have saved Allicin? She had planned a dinner out, followed by an early return to the house. Then, Judy and Allicin could get to know Marc. It had all gone wrong with that knock on the door. She must forget "that", and think of Allicin. Allicin could stay with Aunt Nell in Groton for the time being.

Judy mentioned this to Marc, and the arrangements where agreed upon.

In Preparation for her date with Marc she had taken Allicin over to her baby sitter's. June now returned with Allicin. Judy rushed to the front steps to meet them. She(Judy) avoided a lot of questions from both of them by her quick interception on the steps. Judy asked June to take Allicin over to Aunt Nell in Groton. She gave June directions to the house, and said she would call Nell to explain. Judy told June that she couldn't explain to her now, but would explain at a more convenient time.

June said she understood, and would call the following day.

Allicin asked, "where was Marc?"

Judy responded with a kiss and a hug. You will see Marc another time. Go with June to Aunt Nell, and I will call later.

June took Allicin's hand, waved, and they left.

Marc now took Judy to see Mrs. Vincinto at the boarding house. The room was on a corner of the second floor. Marc's door was two doors down the hall. The room was clean and neat, and had two windows. One window faced the street, and the other faced a vacant lot next door. Not pretty, but adequate for the time being.

Judy's temporary accommodation was met, so Marc took Judy out for a bite to eat. This was not what Marc had in mind earlier, but it would have to suffice.

Judy was exhausted from her ordeal so they soon returned to the boarding house immediately after their repast.

Marc kissed Judy lightly on the lips while saying "good night."

Judy responded with a quick hug.

Marc assured her he would be near at hand.

With tears in her eyes Judy thanked Marc for everything.

"Good night Marc my Champion," Judy said as she closed her door.

Marc returned to his room and practiced Chi Kung and T'ai Chi for two hours. He then retired, relaxed from the affects of the soothing Internal Arts. He would drop Judy off at work in the morning. He would then go directly to the police station.

Chapter 6

Protectors Of The Publics Rights

Marc entered the grimy city police station with the hope of some quick action by the locals. He was greeted by an empty information desk. Marc did see four policeman playing poker at the rear of the reception area.

Marc inquired, "to whom should I report an assault and break-in too"? No one answered so Marc repeated the question, but this time a little louder.

"Wait a minute buddy, I'll be with you in a minute." This was the reply from a burly Sergeant at the end of the table, the one with the poor poker hand in front of him!

Marc waited a full ten minutes, and then repeated the question for the third time. The question was even louder, and a bit raucous.

The second reply from the sergeant was loud and insistent in return! "What is your problem mister?" Sergeant Bill Rankel was getting annoyed with this stranger. "I told you I'd be with you in a minute, and I will!"

"Hold on" thought Marc to himself, for he saw a problem in the making! Marc turned and started to leave. Marc's turning seemed to instill action into the big sergeant's body.

Rankel got up from his poor five card hand of draw poker and approached Marc.

"Hey you wait a minute," ordered 'the big boy in blue!"

Marc's response was, "thanks, but I'll handle it!"

Sergeant Bill Rankel couldn't believe his ears! Who was this man now facing him, who would handle police matters by himself?

'What's your name, and what's your problem," Rankel inquired angrily?

Marc had turned, only to be confronted with a big, irate, and confused police officer.

A case of pacification Marc thought as he gestured and said, "Wait, hold on, I can explain!"

Rankel grabbed Marc's shirt, and pushed him against the wall.

Marc was flabbergasted, but in reflex action his left hand instantly grasped Rankel's left wrist in a crushing viselike grip.

It was Rankel's turn to be surprised!

Marc was now committed to a course of action that he neither wanted, or could stop!

Rankel, in a painful rage brought his other hand up to release Marc's tortuous grasp on his numbed wrist and forearm. With lightning speed Marc grabbed Rankel's right wrist. He now slipped his hands from Rankel's numbed wrists to his fingers, forcing a pained Rankel into a near by seat!

Marc immediately released the confused Rankel's bent fingers. He apologized with, "it must be my instilled military training", and quickly left the unusual scene.

The incident happened so quickly that the other officers seemed rooted to their seats.

As Marc got into his car he thought gloomily, "the road to hell is now being paved with misplaced good intentions!"

As Marc left the police parking lot he saw one of the poker players taking his license plate number. Was this a portent of things to come?

Chapter 7

Opening Practice

The following weeks after the assault on Judy went by quickly. Until the fall semester and football practice "try-outs" for new students. The regular team was already in practice for five weeks. On the day of the "try-outs", the last lecture on "Morality and Power" was given by Dean Anders. Judy had joined the class to be near Marc. After the class Marc drove Judy back to the apartment.

Marc excused himself from accepting an invitation to go in for refreshments, with the "half excuse" he needed some exercise(this was partially true). He kissed her, and drove away without another word.

Marc drove to the first football try-out practice of the season.

The air was crisp and clean as Marc got out of the Cariera at the football scrimmage field. He thought, "what appropriate weather for the precise surgical operation he had in mind for someone!"

Marc went to the locker room and changed into sweat shirt and sweat pants. He added something from his "black belt" days, wrist straps for added power!

When Marc walked onto the football field Josh Logan felt vindicated. The turn of events was now going in his favor. With a little intimidation this Trembley falls right into line, and his girl friend had been "good at it" to boot!

Coach Jeb Stewart looked over the group of new "recruits", and spotted Marc. This must be the man he had interest in from the application forms scrutiny. In *fact Logan had pointed out the fact that this Trembley seemed to fit the bill for a strong "end", or "half-back".*

It looked like Logan might be right. He assessed the man to be about six to six feet one, and about one hundred and eighty five pounds of solid muscle, and trim as a race horse.

Coach Jeb Stewart thought that a little warm-up was in order. This would allow him to see what kind of shape the veterans were in, as well as the recruits! He started with run and jumps, followed by a four forty yard run. Stewart was surprised to see Trembley whiz smoothly past the recruits and most of the veterans. Trembley ran, not like a racehorse, but like something he'd seen hunting. He had it, it was the puma tracking his deer!

Trembley was becoming an interesting subject to Stewart. He decided to try the strength department next.

"Give me fifty push-ups", called the coach to his behemoths. Everyone did this with ease.

"Give me one hundred push-ups", was the next command. The drop-off started now, with about half the squad left.

One hundred and fifty was next. Only Logan and Trembley remained.

Two hundred would be the final punishment. Logan and Trembley were left, but Logan looked as if he had played sixty minutes of a football game without any breaks.

The coach stopped the contest at a "merciful" two hundred.

"This Mr. Marc Trembley is one hell of an athlete", thought Coach Jeb Stewart. Amazing how easily he did these exercises, and with comparative ease and good rhythm.

The scrimmage came next. Coach Stewart decided to put Trembley into the lineup as the opposing fullback to Logan and the veteran first team.

The veteran guard on the other team was none other than Josh Logan. Logan normally played fullback, but was filling in as guard.

The first play called for the fullback to pass through left guard while the left halfback would block the left tackle. Marc hurtled through the left side, and saw Logan's two hundred and twenty five pounds(or more) bearing down on him in a collision course. Marc shifted to the right with catlike swiftness, but so did Logan! Logan came after Marc as if he was stalking a mouse he was about to crush. Marc suddenly turned toward Logan, and went straight at him. Marc was now running fast, but also very low. Logan leapt for Marc just as Marc's shoulders smashed into Logan's thighs like a freight train hitting a barrier. Marc straightened up with all the power of his legs, shoulders, and arms.

This action threw the gasping Logan over Marc and onto his back. Marc landed on top of him in a thundering mass of crashing bone and muscle.

The coach couldn't believe what he was seeing. A veteran two hundred and twenty eight pound football player flipped over by a hundred and eighty five pound untested rookie player!

The wind was knocked out of Logan for only a few seconds. When he recovered he was mad as hell, and looking for blood. The misplaced fullback got up, clenched his teeth, and drove his right hand into his left to vent his total, frustration and disgust! The next play called for Marc to block for the right halfback. Next he was to do an end run around the right end. Logan came at Marc with fire in his eyes. Logan's fire was extinguished when Marc's head collided with his stomach.

While Logan was falling Marc hit him in the ribs with a fast Judo punch. Logan went out this time, for a full five minutes.

Logan refused to leave the game. He said he simply stumbled, an obvious lie to anyone who was close enough to see the action. The play got a first down because Logan had been put out of commission(temporarily).

The next play again called for Marc to execute an end run. Marc easily cleared the guard and then the opposing end, but he was surprised to see Logan catching up to him. Logan was faster than Marc had thought. Logan caught up to Marc at the ten yard line. Logan threw his forearm at Marc's head. Still holding the ball in his left hand Marc was able to deflect the blow. The heel of Marc's right hand shot up to catch Logan squarely on the chin. The head of Logan snapped back like a toothpick. If Logan didn't have strong neck and shoulder muscles his neck probably would have snapped! Josh Logan collapsed as if he had been shot by a three fifty seven magnum.

Before anyone could get to the ten yard line Marc said, "this is for Judy, stay away or you are dead meat!"

After the "score" Marc came back to the sidelines showing concern for the battered, but wiser Logan.

Coach Stewart watched the entire episode, including the rugged last act. He began to realize that Mr. Marc R. Trembley was more than an athlete, but what?

This was not a game to Trembley, but a lesson in destruction.

Stewart's amazement continued, as Marc led the scratch squad of recruits to a defeat of the first string team!

After the scrimmage Marc apologized to Stewart for "hitting" Logan so hard. He also decided that football was not for him, and left.

Coach Jeb Stewart was amazed again, for Trembley was probably the best athlete he had ever seen!

The coach thought back to the stories he heard about Trembley saving a child from under the wheels of an eighteen wheeler. He had also heard a rumor of a thief being felled with one karate chop.

This man was different than any he had known. Marc Trembley began to remind Stewart of his instructor of hand to hand combat in the Marines. That must be it he thought, combat trained, with martial arts or commando training. "My God, thought Stewart, this man really is deadly!"

Chapter 8

Re-Evaluation

In a mood of contemplation after the events of the last few days Marc thought that re-evaluation of his situation would be in order. Marc thought that his reputation was probably being established as a "ruffian", and not as a student. I must change this image or leave the "halls of higher learning", Marc mused. Marc's military and intelligence training always seemed to lead him into a kind of tactical evaluation of situations. This was no exception. Would a complete change of tactics help, How would he change a lifetimes habits?

Marc's contemplations were interrupted by the phones incessant ring.

"Hello", Marc answered.

"Is this Gary Grantillo?", the hesitant voice of a man asked. ?

"No", Marc answered.

"Who is this", he asked?

"Sorry", said the voice at the other end of the line. He then hung up the phone.

An uneasy feeling came over Marc that he knew the caller. Paranoia setting in thought Field Rep. #321.

Setting his mind back to planning, the situation seemed a bit hopeless! The soft touch and hard line hadn't worked, so what now? Maybe it took more, or *possibly less than an attitude change. Would just a change of clothes work? He could try something like wearing glasses to look more studious. He could carry a briefcase, wear cords and loafers, a loose fitting psychedelic long sleeved shirt, and wear a beard! Would he then be a nondescript student of the sixties? Would this surface change really work?*

Disguises were not new to Marc, he had used them in Central America, and Europe with some success.

His number two change must be more profound, he must put his "yin" and "yang" in total harmony. He had let external forces overcome his inner control. He must get his "chi" in balance.

Number three, he must put out "feelers" to the intelligence community, and check for any activity in the college community. Too many times he had seen the slightest discrepency from the norm indicating surveillance activities presence!

Mark's recollections went back to his "recruitment" by the CIA's Station Chief for the Golden Triangle, Major John Robello. Mark was the Senior Instructor for a tactical operations group. The instruction centered on using martial arts in unarmed combat. Mark had just been assigned to the unit. He was observing the instruction given by a sergeant.

The sergeant was showing some veterans how to take-down an opponent with a knife.

Mark had no identification of name, rank, or insignia about him. He was attired in camouflage pants, and a green "T" Shirt. He had no boots on.

He watched as a canny corporal got through the sergeants feint and block, and cut into his shoulder! The sergeant was stunned, but before the corporal could deliver the coup-de-tat, Mark moved with a tigers grace from the corporals right side. He grabbed the corporals right knife hand wrist with his right hand. Mark was going with the thrusts momentum. Then he reversed the direction of movement by twisting and jerking the mans wrist and arm back to his shoulder. Marc's left arm striking under the mans left arm pit and chest forcing the man over his out stretched leg. The corporal was hurled onto his back. The force of impact sent the knife flying from his immobilized hand and wrist. A quick and measured karate chop to the temple put the corporal out cold.

"Hello, I'm Major John Robello! That was quite a demonstration. I'd like to have a talk with you. Are you game?"

"I'm game for almost anything that's legal" exclaimed Mark!

Robello and Trembley walked away from the training area to have a chat that would affect a life time!

Robello was a very good "pitch man". His pitch revolved around getting a tough and dirty job done for the love of country, the service, and especially pride in oneself. He also stressed that few men, if any, could qualify to do the job. Robello slyly quoted other candidates (such as Captain Cheston) he knew Mark admired.

Robello's timing was perfect. Mark was on a plateau for work assignments and advancement. After a third hitch, it was decision time. But, now he had another option! An alternate solution? Or was it from frying pan into the fire?

Mark's mind went back to another choice, but this "choice" had been made for him. His father had made it!

His mind went back to his disturbing childhood. With stark clarity he remembered his fathers brutal treatment of his mother. He could see his drunken fathers big figure looming over him again! His fists were closed, but so were his nine year old boy's!

Bruce Trembley could hardly believe his eyes! His nine year old kid Mark was ready to do battle with him, Bruce Trembley!

His kid had guts, whatever kind of brat he was he could take it! Bruce Trembley hit Mark one more time, for good luck! He couldn't believe his nine year old would take on his father at one ninety five!

"Damn it", if the kid wanted to fight he'd teach him a lesson. Bruce Trembley wouldn't have his kid talking back and fighting his dad. He would enroll him in the toughest Martial Arts course he could find! He would find out just how tough this brat kid of his was!

It took three hard years, but the satisfaction remained to this day about his triumph on returning. His father was now ill, and most of the bully had receded with the loss of his great strength. He could still see his fathers astonished face when he entered the room and presented his father with the belt. It was black. This was only one of many belts young Mark Trembley would acquire in military, and in civilian venues.

Thinking of Robello, Mark's mind searched his memory for clues to the allusive major's past until it began to loom close to the surface of Marc's consciousness in vivid reality. The man was speaking in broken English with heavy Spanish accent. He was angry, very angry. "The Agency was to send us the other man to organize the guerrillas into striking teams!", he said. "No one showed up! The government forces are due to arrive any minute, you help?" The Captain's mind raced over the only facts available. His counterpart Major John Robello had formed the guerrillas into striking teams. But, no one had showed up! The government forces arrival were eminent. The Captain was new to this area of the world, so he might as well have been "green"!

"What were Major Robello's instructions?" asked the Captain of the scared Central American.

When no answer came, the Captain looked at the area "commandidos", and noticed one who looked American! He now directed his question to this man.

"What were Major Robello's last instructions?"

The clipped British accent took the Captain by surprise! "It would not be cricket to go to the rallying area at this-time as it would be particularly dangerous."

"Who the hell are you?" demanded the Captain.

"A man who is working as your counterpart, and Major John Robello's replacement," came the reply.

"Are you classified for this project?" Marc asked.

"Yes, all the way," replied SAS Major Robert Elliott Robertson.

Marc got the distinct impression that more than a military mission was involved here. What was an English mercenary doing in the jungles of Central America?

Marc was suddenly brought from his recollections to the present with a knock on the door.

Marc walked over to the window and looked out before going back to open the door. He noticed that the man in the back seat of the ever present Trans-Am seemed to be missing. Marc opened the door with a quick jerk, and grabbed the man in a business suit, then grabbed the man's knocking hand. Turning the hand in a clockwise motion he applied moderate pressure to the elbow forcing the man to the floor. The man gasped and cursed in painful moanings. Almost as an automatum, Marc rolled on top of the man placing his knee on the spine, and twisted the right arm back to his shoulder blades. He then pulled the chin back, but only to the point of some tensioning of the neck, throat, and shoulder muscles.

He gasped "Reach into my . . .", exploded from the desperate man's throat!

Marc let go of the head, and reached into the terrified mans inner coat pocket. The familiar ASA Insignia on the ID in the wallet was acknowledged, then thrown aside by Marc.

Marc now felt for a weapon, but found none.

The mans face was turning an ashen color, so Marc released his painful hold of the arm.

The man was still aghast at what had happened to an experienced ASA Investigator, when Marc pulled him to his feet.

Marc apologized saying that it was a rough place to live and you couldn't be to careful with the crime rate as high as it is.

Lieutenant Arthur Roscoe of the ASA tried to compose himself, and to get his attention focused on this formidable adversary! Roscoe's "cover" as a hotel inspector was now blown to pieces(it wasn't very good in the first place).

The units Commander Major Clem Colson had only warned Roscoe to be careful, not that the man could be so lethal. (Roscoe knew that he had been spared, and that he could have been dead.) He would find out(too late) that Trembley was a black belt in two external martial arts, and a "master" in an internal form.

The confidential military note indicated that he was proficient in the "field use" of all three. This usually meant that he was deadly accurate in all forms.

There was nothing for Roscoe to do, but to come clean with Trembley. He told Marc of the concern for him at the university. Dean Anders call had set lots of machinery in motion.

Clem Colson had been the recipient of a CIA "prompt" call from a MR. Alton. Alton said, "that Trembley was a man he wanted watched, but to avoid him(the last part Colson had neglected to mention to Roscoe as well).

Marc told Roscoe that he had had a little trouble, but nothing that he wanted to hide from the CIA, ASA, or anyone else for that matter.

Roscoe seemed only too happy to accept Marc's explanation. So this ended the matter.

The two men shook hands, and Roscoe left the building.

Sorrier, but wiser for the encounter!

Chapter 9

John Robello

Marc watched the rumpled Lt. Arthur Roscoe get into the black Trans-Am, and then it sped away. Marc's mind was becoming increasingly focused on the intelligence community, and his present and former relationship to it. The feeling was not particularly comfortable. Perhaps it was time for him to reacquaint himself with some of his old friends and buddies. This must be done for preservation's sake, and not for prudence's sake.

First things first thought Marc as the first pangs of hunger began to reshape his priorities. Judy, and certainly Marc needed more than a fast food "livery stable" to satisfy his horses appetite! Rather than walk, he decided to take the car so that he could look for a really nice place.

Marc dressed in conservative sports clothes, but added his derringer as added attire. This deadly friend was enclosed in a small leather case, which fit neatly into his inside coat pocket.

Too many coincidences were beginning to add up, but to what? He didn't know yet, but he would endeavor to find out for sure!

As he left Marc left a thin piece of twine across the door. He placed it at the bottom, about a foot above the sill.

With a few precautions in place Marc was just a little bit happier as he proceeded to Judy's room for their date. He called her name, and rapped on the door at the same time. Her soft voice ushered him into her room. He was totally *unprepared for Judith McPherson. Standing before him across the room was five feet of beauty, and a sight too behold it was! Her light pink blouse of Japanese design was silk, seductive, and form fitting. Her green pleated skirt had a matching coat folded neatly over the end of the bed. Her red hair and light makeup complemented the lovely apparition before him. A thin gold chain hung around her neck. Marc was simply overwhelmed.*

He was proud and delighted to escort this lovely lady to a restaurant of her choice. Judy suggested French Cuisine at a place in downtown Needham.

Judy was secretly pleased that her closeness caused such discomfort to Mr. Marc Trembley! She was beginning to play cat and mouse with this strong man of action. She suspected that Marc enjoyed the game, but didn't let on that he did.

Marc Trembley on the other hand, was beginning to realize that his distraction from potential danger, was not academic, but feminine in nature! His training and long experience as an operative must be wearing off.

A light rain was falling gently as the couple left the boarding house.

Now that Marc was focusing on his nemesis, he could hopefully counter it with increased caution and foresight!

Glancing to his left and then right as they descended the stairs Marc noted with interest some irregularities on the street.

A teenage boy was throwing a brand new tennis ball against a wall, but the wall or sidewalk had no boundaries drawn on them!

A blue Mercur XR4TI with the engine running was parked about a half a block from the boarding house. The driver was a man in a business suit who looked out of place in this working class neighborhood. He was idle until he spotted Judy and Marc. He then took a paper off the seat, and began to scan it.

It was odd to have a completely deserted street with no cars and one boy throwing a ball!

This tranquil scene was just too much for Marc!

Marc guided a protesting Judy back into the boarding house hall.

A plan of action was in the making for the new Mr. Cautious. The Porsche couldn't be used because it was too close to the Mercur.

The back door was probably being watched.

Marc decided to take Judy further from any potential action. He took her back to her room.

Judy protested profusely saying that Marc was overprotective and paranoid. Marc prevailed. Marc leveled with her about the possibilities and probabilities of trouble being fairly high! He instructed her to keep the door locked until he returned.

Marc was very happy that Allicin was still at her Aunts. At least this complication wouldn't hinder his actions.

He returned to his own room and changed into running "togs". He slipped a roll of quarters into his right pocket, along with his car keys. The derringer wouldn't be necessary, as surprise and stealth would be his only weapons!

The stealthy figure of Marc moved down the hallway and on to the fire escape quickly and easily. He went down the ladder, and then moved to the alley at a quickening pace. Marc Trembley reached the street at a slow run. He headed straight toward the boy with the ball. As he passed the boy, he snatched the tennis ball, and then stumbled. The startled boy came after him yelling about the new ball he had just been given!

This pretty well confirmed Marc's suspicions! He turned, stopped, and returned the ball to the exasperated but happy boy.

Marc now jogged toward the Mercour at a rapid pace. He saw one man with his coat off sitting on the passengers side. His suit coat was folded across the drivers seat.

As Marc got to the car he collapsed in a bath of sweat on the hood of the Mercour!

The startled man got out of the car, and ran into a stiff right cross. His body caved in, but Marc caught him before he could hit the ground. Marc wrestled the unconscious man's dead weight onto the back seat of the car.

Marc now explored the vehicle for a clue as to the man's identification. In the left-hand coat pocket of the suit coat he found the telltale ID he expected to find(ASA)! Under the driver's seat was a government issue thirty eight automatic.

And surprise, surprise, when Marc turned on the radio he heard running water, and even Judy's voice humming! Marc reached under the dashboard and partially pulled all the plug-in connections, just to make it interesting!

Marc then extracted the clip from the automatic, along with two spares, and put them into his sweat pants pockets.

The agent started to wake up, but Marc put him back to sleep with a quick karate chop to the neck. This would be a long troubled sleep for this poor agent of Uncle Same!

Marc now locked the doors to the car with the agent's own keys, and then put them into his pocket.

He then returned to the boarding house and proceeded to change back into sports clothes again. He went to Judy's room to collect her, and try to bolster her confidence with assurances that all was well again!

Judy was not at all convinced that all was well again, but she had come to trust this man of compassion and power instinctively.

After a pause to reflect, Marc put his arm around Judy's waist and walked her down the front stairs, and deposited her in the front seat of the Porsche. As the Porsche passed the Mercour the groggy agent was trying to put things together.

He literally didn't know what hit him!

Marc chuckled when he thought what "control" would have to say to this red faced agent! Of particular interest would be the package he would be sending to Langley.

The couple arrived at Shamus restaurant in Needham at about eight thirty. The sky was clear, and the air was clean from the recent rain.

The maitre-d showed them to a table to the rear, and away from the floor show. The show was about to begin with a duet called "Ron and Penny". The crowd was talkative, but orderly. As they wove through the tables Marc thought he saw a familiar body outlined at the bar, and to the side.

Major John Robello was not too happy with this rendezvous. He sat at the bar drinking whiskey, and thinking unhappy thoughts about his "needs"! Yet, he could remember in past Special Forces and CIA forays his pleasure in the completion of a nasty assignment. He remembered in particular the bogus rewards of women, money, and good times. Back to the present things were not too good. He had been buying weapons and mercenaries, but couldn't find a leader for his little cadre of death!
   Patriotism, nationalism, greed, fear, or hunger had not given him the leader for this deadly group of mercenaries! Some of the lower order "boys" had feelers out for two officers from the "Red Group". There was a hint of trouble from sources close to these men.

Robello told "control" that he preferred John Cheston to Marc Trembley. They were both good, but Trembley was too straight for his liking!

Robello had authorization that was almost carte-blanche in scope for this highly classified operation. The operation consisted(in part) of destabilizing foreign governments that were not sympathetic or politically correct to ours. Robello well knew that the company would put it's own interpretation on the methods and agenda to be used. He also knew that it would not be a "cakewalk" to use the vernacular(Even for the elite "Red Group")! He knew that Captains Cheston and Trembley had the unique cunning, technical expertise, physical stature, and dogged patriotism to carry out this tricky destabilization of a country. But, he had to admit that that Trembley had an edge. Trembley was an incredible martial artist in three disciplines. Cheston had only one Black Belt! Part of Trembley's problem was his individualistic operational methods. It was documented that one of his "Controls" didn't like this one little bit either! His superior had also indicated that if Trembley was used and he disappeared, that would be a satisfactory outcome!

Robello was nursing his whiskey sour, when he noticed the couple being seated to his right. The man with the beautiful redhead had some familiar qualities about him! Robello looked closer as they were seated, and looked straight into the deep blue eyes of Captain Marc Trembley!

Instant recognition and a surprised expression registered on Marc's face.

A chill came over Marc as he thought of the possibilities of why this "deceased" agent was sipping his whiskey with no apparent ill affects, even from death itself!

Marc recalled the story of Robello as the leader of two CIA Teams being shot, possibly by his own men!

Judy noticed that Marc's face had become a kind of hardened/chiseled outline, and that his color was almost bloodless. Her blue eyes followed Marc's gaze to the big man seated at the bar with the two Asians. He was staring back at Marc, and a grin was beginning to fill his hard round face. The man made Judy uneasy, as he seemed to emanate an aura of danger and cynicism.

Judy again looked at Marc, and his tensed body and chiseled features had miraculously relaxed and softened!

She again looked at the man at the bar, and he had also changed like a chameleon and now appeared normal.

Marc spoke first. "Judy, order for us both, and I'll be right back." As he spoke, Marc got up and headed for the man at the bar, who it turned out to be was Robello!

"Very short funeral", Marc commented as he shook the extremely healthy Major's hand!

"Can we talk?" Marc commented as he surveyed the two Asians.

Robello appraised one of the final "Group Leader" Candidates with extreme interest, and some apprehension.

The fact that Trembley was dating the "girl next door" type, and even attending college again made this tough veteran very uneasy.

He would have been happier if Trembley was whoring it up, and was in real trouble with the authorities. Yet, Captain Marc Trembley had been decisive in his actions, but had not used "deadly force", as yet that is!

John Robello laughed when he thought of the gauntlet that the former Captain Marc Trembley would be entering. He would find out what Trembley was made of, and it had better be cold hard steel!

Robello introduced the Asian to his right as Yang Ti. He would not be introduced to the other man, probably a Korean by his looks and carriage.

Marc noted the omission. He also noted the combat hard look of the man. Definitely this was a man to be avoided. Mr. X was a tall five foot ten by Korean standards. His build was athletic, but not stocky and over muscled. His clothes were casual and loose fitting. He looked ready for anything, or anybody.

John Robello made it a point to know everything about enemies, friends, associates, and possible adversaries! And, he already knew Marc R. Trembley, the Captain of Special Forces like a brother!

John ordered his own favorite whisky sour #3, and Marc's favorite, a black Russian Vodka.

Robello took the initiative and headed off Marc's questions with a quick explanation, and questions of his own! On our last job in Central America with the "Red Team", I was lucky to have Kim to back me up! He(Kim) got me out before government troops ambushed me! But, enough of that.

Marc glanced at the Korean. He gave a slight grin with a dip to the shoulders, indicating acknowledgment! So, Marc surmised, the Korean Kim must be Robello's right arm!

At this stage Marc thought he should assess Kim's potential! His height was about five foot nine. His weight was approximately a hundred and seventy five pounds. The man's build looked to be well muscled, but not to the extent of weight lifting. His speed and timing would be very fast. These would be his ultimate weapon. His repertoire of martial arts would probably include Tar-Kwon-Do(the standard

Korean Art), Karate, Jiu-Jitsu, and possibly one of the eclectic systems. His capabilities probably didn't include one of the Internal(or soft) systems or Metaphysical Boxing. All in all this was a very dangerous little man! Marc laughed a dry laugh to himself. This little oriental has the perfect center of gravity to excel in any martial art!

John Robello on the other hand didn't have to assess the capabilities of Marc Trembley, yet! Trembley had already passed Robello's preliminaries, but the question remained would Trembley pull the trigger again?

Marc was brought back from his musing's by another question from the Major.

"Marc, could you make yourself available for a small, easy, and profitable operation?"

Marc was irritated that he was being hustled by a man who had essentially left him to take the blame for an operation that Robello himself had fouled up! Marc had been left in the lurch, and innocent people had died! With utter exasperation for any proposal from Robello Marc slammed his fist down on the bar. Marc's drink went flying spilling its contents over Kim, and a brute of a man next to him.

Kim didn't flick an eye, but the big man was furious! The man lunged for Marc while spewing obscenities about Marc and his family! That was as far as he got. Kim's legs shot out and toppled the poor smuck! Before he could gain his balance, again Kim acted. Kim's right and left arms came down in lightning Karate chops to both shoulders, temporarily paralyzing the mans upper body! He crashed to the floor in agonizing pain.

Robello's voice raged over the turmoil. "No more Kim, no more!"

Kim withdrew both arms to his chest, with palms down. He then shifted his weight back to both legs, then dropped his hands to his sides. Luckily the precise and deadly kicks did not come, and he would survive!

With sweat on his brow Marc exclaimed, "thanks, Kim!"

A bow from Kim followed, along with a slight correction. I am not Kim, I am Yaung!

"Thanks Yaung" Marc said with some amusement.

The bar was in an uproar. The bartender had ducked behind the bar. Women were screaming that a man had been killed. Men and women alike had moved out of the range of the violent scene.

Robello was again barking an order to all and sundry, "Get out before the local police arrive!"

In the midst of the confusion Marc yelled his answer back to Robello, "no to your offer, I am out of it for good!"

Robello and company left by the side door just as the police arrived through the front door. Leading the charge was none other than Marc's 'friend' Sergeant Bill Rankel!

Marc sat down beside the scared Judy. She had been glued to her chair during the entire episode.

Chapter 10

Asa's Renewed Contact

Marc reached across the table and held Judy's hands in the powerful envelope of his own hands. He caressed her hands with his fingers, which began to relax her whole body. Her face became less tense. Judy's body relaxed into a smooth and tender outline of loveliness.

This serene moment was a captured moment in time interrupted by the harsh voice of Sergeant Bill Rankel!

"What to hell is going on here?", demanded an irritated Rankel! Who assaulted this white guy here? Why doesn't someone speak up?

The other two offices started walking through the isles between the tables looking for the perpetrators of the assault. They walked right past the loving couple.

Rankel looked around and saw an old "friend", none other then Mr. Marc Trembley!

The bartender who had been strangely quiet exclaimed, "he's one of the troublemakers, he's the one"!

Rankel stormed over to Marc's table, but backed off a bit when he saw the beautiful redhead sitting at the table with him!

"All right Trembley, what happened here, and what is your involvement in it?"

As Rankel was speaking the other two police officers moved in on the other side of Marc.

A cool and self satisfied Rankel told the two officers to handcuff this dangerous man. He said that he(Rankel) had encountered this man Trembley before, and Trembley had been violent.

Marc let the two officers put his wrists together, and to "cuff" them. He must restrain himself and play "a waiting game"!

A sarcastic smile of relief crossed Sergeant Bill Rankel's face. He finally had Trembley where he wanted him.

Judy now questioned Rankel! "What are you doing sergeant? Marc has done nothing! I saw the whole thing, do you want facts, or are you seeking vengeance?"

All thirty people in the restaurant bar were watching with jaundiced eyes. "Leave the man alone, he did nothing. It was the Korean", several volunteered.

Rankel was hot under the collar, but no fool! He bowed to the dictates of public sentiment, and witnesses thereof!

He now softened his strident position, and actually started to investigate the incident.

"Who else saw what happened?", he asked! Five men and one woman came forward to give their stories. It was too many confirming stories for Rankel to ignore. He took the handcuffs off Marc, but gave him strong warning to stay out of trouble, or else!

Marc's sarcasm was almost involuntary. "I'm truly sorry sergeant, I'll stay away from rough crowds in the future, sir!"

Marc was beginning to enjoy the theatrics of the moment, and turned with a flare. With a wave Marc began to leave, but Rankel stuck his big foot out, and tripped Marc. The instant he felt he was falling Marc flipped his body forward in a tight forward somersault. He barely made it all the way over, even with a tremendous thrust of his torso. As Marc straightened out his upper body, he grabbed a glass of beer off the nearest table. Marc raised his glass in a toast to the "good Sergeant Rankel". He then raised his glass to the whole assemblage!

Judy seized the moment to join Marc in the isle. They quickly left through the main entrance.

They could hear the laughter through the closing door, and they knew that made Rankel furious!

Judy was beginning to wonder if Marc looked for trouble, or if trouble followed him around with a vengeance! The confrontations. and incidents were becoming commonplace. She knew in her heart that she was more than a friend, but what of Allison? All this violence was not good for a child to see. Questions would be raised by relatives and friends about the whole situation. Judy would have to get Allison and return to her house.

They sat in the car relaxing after leaving the bar. Mark could see that Judy was deep in thought. He didn't disturb her thoughts, but drove to the nearest "golden arches" for some long delayed fast food. As they sat eating burgers and fries Marc's sixth sense told him to be careful! Watch your back remember your teachers saying, "that the enemy you can't see is the most dangerous!" Now his instinct took over, and he began to adhere to it's tenets. His sixth sense was almost always correct. Looking around he was relieved to see the usual family crowd and a sprinkling of couples scattered through out "Big Mac's Place."

Marc now focused on Judy because he could see that she was very upset. "Not the quiet meal in a romantic setting we had hoped for", said Marc in his softest voice.

Judy began to speak in her soft tones with pregnant pauses between emphasized words. "Don't get me wrong Marc I'm very fond of you", she explained. It is very nice to be escorted by a strong man who is also a gentleman. But, I must think of Allison and her future. I don't quite know how to explain to a young child why you have to use deadly force on another individual, who after all is a human being! How can I explain that every time we go out something awful happens?

Marc's mind drifted back to Dung Ho, and the time the unit he was training got ambushed by a Viet Cong Company. It was a particularly vicious fight. The American's superior automatic weapons helped by open terrain spelled success at the final count for the US trainees.

After the firefight Marc laid down his M16 to give aid to a wounded comrade at the outer perimeter of the skirmish. Marc went to assist the man who was lying near a clump of bushes. Just as he reached the corporal, he realized that his weapon was over twenty yards from it's owner(A no-no to a recruit, never mind a seasoned instructor.) At close range he could see that the soldier had been garroted, and that he was long dead! With his good peripheral vision he caught a bright reflection coming from his left. He also heard some movement from his immediate right.

Something whizzed over Marc's head. Instantly Marc dropped back onto his shoulders, and with a simultaneous thrust of his feet back and up he made contact with something! With a terrible thud and a screech the black clad figure was hit at the breastplate just below the neck. The VC's body shot back and up in a tortured arc of convulsion. Marc now rolled to his right just as a silver blade made an impression where his body had been in the dirt just a moment before! He now rolled back hand entwined two black pajama legs in his own, toppling the man to the damp soil. with lightning speed the Green Beret forced his knee into the VC's spine. He grasped the man's head and twisted sharply, and the guerrilla's spine snapped with a sickening crack. Marc turned over and flipped to his feet and a crouching position. The next attacker came from his right. With a quick but effortless block he deflected the knife down and away from his body. Marc's weight now shifted from his left to his right leg as he simultaneously stepped forward clasping the armpit with his left hand and driving his handblade under the VC's ribcage. As the attacker pitched forward with an agonizing scream Marc brought the withdrawn right hand, palm out in an uppercut that had his legs and shoulders driving upward. The body went up and down in a short arc of death. This was a North Vietnamese Regular who landed a few feet from Marc. His head was twisted to one side, grotesquely broken! The Special Forces Captain settled his body back into a semi-crouch with legs-shoulder width apart, and evenly balanced, preparing for the next attack, but it didn't come!

When it was apparent that the attacks were over he relaxed his karate "horse stance", and resumed his normal posture.

Quickly he examined the communist soldiers. Two were dead, but one was living. The remaining man was a strong but groggy VC. He came at Marc with his bayonet. In a T'ai Chi Chaun "Grasping The Sparrows Tail Move" Marc incorporated an improvisation. Instead of grasping the elbow, he grasped the wrist with his right hand and chopped the elbow with his left handblade. He broke the elbow. The black clad figure writhing in pain was now hit with a powerful foot thrust to the groin. He was spun over onto his back by the force of the kick. He lay there in agony now helpless to further attack Marc!

When Marc's thoughts came back to the present he realized that Judy was right. He would have to be celibate and cleanse the dangerous environment around him of all the distracting influences that his present life seemed to encompass. So, this "Wisdom Seeker" would have to wait and the black belted carnivore would now stake and cleanse his territory.

With moist eyes Judy watched the one she loved decide on a tangent to the life she knew he desperately wanted to take! She knew that this was necessary in order to facilitate a solution to his many problems from the past.

They both knew that until these problems were solved separation was inevitable.

Marc would miss Judy immensely, but he would also miss the chance to see Allison grow from the wonders of childhood into adulthood.

Marc thought that now he had made the decision to temporarily break up, his main concern would take care of itself. This diversion would work only if he had room to move, and not be worried by concerns about their safety! To facilitate this he would get them back to their house, and in their own safe environment. He would enlist some help to ensure this. He would then distance himself from them completely.

This tough warrior knew that Judy had long since become more than a vulnerable kitten to protect. His instincts were always with the underdog. This had always been his Waterloo, but this was much more, much more! Before Judy he was a very efficient machine, with a heart, but it was almost too hard to penetrate. Judy had done this without his even knowing he had become human again! This violence that permeated his whole being was a leftover that overflowed from his cruel and abused childhood! As a child he had sought refuge from his instantaneous temper in the discipline of the martial arts. That is when he began to internalize his fears and frustrations! And, he had found peace and courage in the molding of mind and body into one.

Marc remembered the stimulation of the progression from child to man. The encompassing of the substantial and insubstantial, the tranquillity of effortless motion, and the action of yielding and unyielding. And always there was the golden thread of discipline that held all martial arts together. With time and application his Yin and Yang came into harmony, and his Chi grew until he became a master. The boy Marc had found his niche, and his home. Complete within himself, he would be "tried" before the "Wisdom Seeker" would come!

Marc pulled himself back to the present. In the present again, he knew he must distance himself from his loved ones. The only way was to be harsh to make a clean break.

Now! The silence of the inevitable encompassed them as the uncaring world swirled about them.

"I'll get two more coffee's to settle our nerves", said Marc. As he got up he noticed the familiar Trans-Am in the third row of the parking lot. Time to break it off with a mood change, he thought. "Dam it Judy, "he said as he returned!" Why can't you be more sympathetic?" Marc's uncharacteristic surly antagonism took Judy by surprise, and she started to cry.

Marc continued the castigation, according to his new plan, and with devastating affect! Judy got up from the table and called a taxi to take her home. She left Big Marc's place in tears, got into the taxi and left Marc. She couldn't understand this kindly man(whom she secretly had come to love) turning on her so quickly! Contrary to all of her feelings about him, Mr. Marc Trembley must have another darker side that he hides from all and sundry! It must be the reason he was in that Special Forces part of the army which seemed to be tearing into their lives now. But, their relationship must end now!

Marc now set at the table. alone, and thought that before the grueling duel begins he would "tie one on", at the nearest bar! He made a mental note that when his personal war begins, it would be fought in "their" home port!

Marc was leaving for the nearest pub, when non other than the ASA'S point man approached from his pretty Trans-Am to greet his new friend!

"Captain Trembley, could I have a few minutes of your time to help "neutralize" our situation", said the ASA'S nervous Arthur Roscoe!

Marc felt sorry for this "cog" in the military's bureaucratic mill, which Marc guessed had dislodged his grip on his career!

"Come on Roscoe, we will discuss this over some libation, and maybe we can find some middle ground to settle on after all!"

"Follow me, until I find a quiet bar or lounge. I'm driving the red Porsche."

They both laughed at the thought that the car Roscoe had been following had to be identified to him, especially by the person being followed! The ease of Roscoe's laugh was tinged with slight trepidation of impending doom.

Using his cellular phone, Roscoe called home base to update the plan to phase #2. The anticipation in the response belied the anger in the voice at the other end.

Marc's red Porsche wound through the streets of the inner city, finally(in desperation) stopping at a dumpy looking place called "Sams Dungeon." As the two cars pulled into the small parking lot, only three spaces were empty. Most of the vehicles were small trucks, with the exception of a Jaguar roadster.

The front door of the dive looked as if a battering ram hadn't quite made it's way through it! The interior was noisy, smoky, and probably filled with reefers, smack, or the like. Not ideal, but it would cover a confidential chat.

Over a tankard of draft beer Roscoe conveyed the message to Marc that, "the ASA will stop following you if you agree to give a little help to the organization, on a consulting basis." The first part would be finding Captain Cheston from the "Red Team" but further details would be forthcoming, but, basically it would entail finding other veterans for recruitment.

Marc's questions were strait and to the point.

"Why are you following me in the first place?"

"Why is the ASA doing the CIA's dirty work?"

Answer these and I might agree to help you. Scratch my back and I'll scratch yours!

Roscoe was visibly relieved to see even the possibility of a settlement with this deadly adversary. But, he could not tell Trembley of the "dues" his boss owed to *a high CIA official. It was more than his job was worth! He knew he was being used as a subordinate means to an end by the CIA. He knew by the vehemence of the overheard conversation that in the end they wanted Marc out of the way! He knew that he must continue with the "script" he had been given for he was just a cog in-the bureaucratic mill. He now delivered his lines!*

"We are following you as a sub-contractor for the CIA. They have some leverage because we had some soldiers who had gone bad. They took care of the situation without any publicity. So, we are paying the favor back by keeping an eye on you. At some time they would contact you directly with the offer I mentioned."

Marc agreed(with his own agenda in mind), but with the realization that any agreement with Intelligence Organizations are tenuous at best! They shook hands on "it". Now, Marc gave Roscoe some friendly advice, namely "watch your back!"

As they were talking Marc noticed that the bar was filling up with more people. The working class crowd was being joined by a better dressed class of people, namely professionals.

"Lets have another for the road," said Marc. "It looks like a long year for both of us!" They drank in silence for a while, and then they got up and left. Several people seemed to follow. Roscoe was getting more nervous by the minute. They parted at the door, each going his own way.

Chapter 11

The CIA's Answer

Marc watched Roscoe's Trans-Am pull away, and noted with apprehension that a big black V8 Oldsmobile pulled out right behind him. He walked over to his Porsche, and noted that it was sitting a bit low on one side. Paranoid, he thought, "what I need is another drink, and to hell with it all." Retracing his steps to the bar, the stale smell of after-shave harassed his nostrils as he entered the door.

Looking at the bar, he noticed three stools to the far left that were vacant. Marc took the one to the far left, sat down and ordered a double vodka. Soldiers were cuddling two bar girls, and to his right two "hard hats" were getting stoned.

Marc now settled into getting soused in the quickest possible time by ordering a second vodka. He gulped it down, and ordered another double from the bemused bartender.

As Marc ordered, the seats next to him filled with two big guys, but Marc drank on!

At the seventh double vodka the former Captain of The Army Marc Trembley decided he was sloshed enough to leave.

Unknown to the inebriated Trembley, his two "neighbors" at the bar left at the same time, and followed him into the parking lot. Four other "business types" left the same bar as well! Just as Marc got to his car he felt the closeness of lurking shadows.

Marc turned, but with the dulled speed of the inebriated state of semi-consciousness. He tried to lower his upper torso, but didn't quite make it. The crashing blow of a fist crashed off the top of his head. A dazed Marc brought his right arm up in a blocking motion, driving the next blow up and away. Marc drove his left fist into the mans left kidney, as the man was turned to the right with the blocking motion. The blow was ineffectual. It did delay the man, but only an instant. It hadn't stopped him by any means!

Marc tried to clear his head, just as another man came around the side of his car with a knife at the ready. He came down with the knife in the usual stabbing motion, but Marc(more alert now) rolled back on his right foot. He simultaneously brought his right hand up, and with his left hand guided the man's arm and body to the right.

Marc then shifted his weight from his right to his left foot, and drove his fist into the mans rib cage with devastating affect. This second attacker smashed against a car, and Marc's fist again found it's mark, but this time in the undefended stomach! The first attacker now came back at Marc. He dove over the second attacker, who had collapsed in front of him. His head drove into Marc's stomach, just as Marc turned sideways and propelled a twisting punch into the small of his back. The actions carried both men from between the parked cars and into the isle of the parking lot. The groaning of the massed antagonists was indicative of the fury of the confrontation. The man's new grip on Marc's throat was beginning to take it's toll. Marc was able to roll over onto his assailant, withdrawing his knee and driving it into the mans groin. The man screamed, and released his grip, while writhing in pain on the tarmac.

Marc jumped to his feet, just as a foot caught him a glancing blow on his shoulder and spun him back to the ground.

The first man of the backup team was about to do his thing on Mr. Marc Trembley. Unfortunately for him, Marc was already spinning to gain his balance, even as he was hit. Therefore this glancing kick had little affect, but to throw Marc off balance and to the ground. When Marc flipped to his feet, two of the other backup team grabbed both of his arms.

Marc was becoming so weak and nauseous that even with his iron will and concentration he was beginning to pass out!

Through his developing "fog" amidst all the commotion Marc thought he heard a diesel or was it a gasoline engine? Did he hear air brakes being applied? His head was now spinning.

They had Marc pinned against a car, and one man with dangling dog tags around his neck began to pummel Marc unmercifully.

Marc began to pass out, when suddenly one of his arms was released. Marc's instinct and training instructed his freed arm to come around, and with the heel of his hand to smash the assailants head onto the hood of the car. This man released his grasp of Marc, and with a desperate attempt to escape, raised his head. Marc's slashing karate chop caught the mans neck in a paralyzing encounter! The man rolled off the hood of the car, either out cold, or dead!

Marc now turned around to see another attacker being thrown against an eighteen wheeler, that he now focused on in the aisle of the parking lot. A big truck driver loomed over the hapless attacker, but no response came from the prostrate figure. The man was out cold from the impact of head on metal.

Marc assessed the situation, and saw no less than five assailants taken out of commission. He also saw two men get into a new T-Bird a few rows up, and speed away.

Rollie Fawcett stepped over the figure by his truck, and looked to see how his friend Marc Trembley was doing with his other assailants. But, no fear, Mr. Marc Trembley had just finished the last attacker.

Marc again felt his hand being shaken loose from his arm by this big, big truck driver.

"How did you find me?" asked Marc in disbelief that he had been rescued.

"This is one of my stops," said Rollie, "I deliver beer. Matter of fact, the deliveries take me throughout the city and suburbs like Langley."

It was like a leak in a dam Marc noted, as his head cleared, once Rollie got started he continued unabated!

It turned out that Rollie was married with five children from five to twenty. His wife had polio, but his two sons and three girls were all healthy and handsome. They all took after their mother, of course!

Marc couldn't figure out if Rollie was trying to cheer him up, or if he was naturally this gregarious. What ever it was he was a hell of an asset, as long as he was on your side that is!

Rollie was feeling real good that he could return the favor to this ferocious "little guy" who had saved the child from his trucks wheels. He was about to make the suggestion that Marc come over to meet the family, when he saw the three men. He tensed at the thought that they might be baddies!

Marc saw them too. They were rugged military types, and Marc recognized them as Special Forces noncoms in the bodies of Dale McAdams, Ralph Johnson, and another man. As Marc had been, they had been on one of the special tactical teams that did the dirty undercover work the headlines never saw.

"Captain Trembley, what happened here?" McAdams inquired. "It looks like you took care of the situation in any case though!" He continued.

McAdams now introduced the others as admirers of the "Blue Team", it's leader John Robello, and of Trembley.

They were obviously surprised to see that Marc had company, and in the large form of Rollie Fawcett! But, the three soldiers recovered their composure quickly.

As the men talked the assailants melted into the streets of the city and disappeared.

"We have been out of the service for four months, and are looking for work", volunteered McAdams.

Now that's funny, thought Marc. If memory serves me right McAdams and Johnson had served two tours of duty and were dedicated to a military career.

As Rollie shook their hands(and bodies), Marc heard the unmistakable sound of dogtags. Marc's antennae went out!

Another alarm bell went out when the other man(John Anders) seemed familiar to Marc, and Marc had never met the man. Strange thought Marc, had I seen his face on a Secret File, or what? The southern "twang" of Dale McAdams again cut through Marc's meandering thoughts like a knife.

"I have some real fine malt liquor back at my place, and would be honored and obliged if you and your friend Rollie here would help me to finish it off! But, if Rollie has to get back to his trucking that is okay also. "Something just didn't figure. How come they were here? Marc hadn't seen them in the bar! Why hadn't they come to the aide of Marc and Rollie? And most importantly, why the dogtags if they were out of the army?

Marc relaxed his whole body with knees slightly bent. His shoulders became soft and rounded. He became very alert, and his eyes focused left and then right.

The blow came unexpectedly from the rear, and not from the soldiers that were visible! It crashed at Marc's head with potentially deadly accuracy.

Marc sank straight down, and caught the arm in a scissors action with his two arms. Marc slid his left hand to the wrist and his right above the elbow and threw the man over his shoulder. Simultaneously Johnson threw a high kick at Marc's head, but the kick caught the flying body(of Marc's adversary from the rear) in mid flight mutually numbing both men.

Marc looked to see where Anders and McAdams were. Anders was out cold on the ground about ten feet from Rollie. Rollie and McAdams were gauging each other with feints and parries.

Marc looked down at Johnson just in time to partially block a single knuckle punch aimed at his rib cage. The blow caught Marc just above the hip, with grimacing pain. He was spun to his left by the blow, but did a 180 turn and drove his right fist in a twisting motion aimed for Johnson's left kidney. Instead it smashed the lower rib cage with enough power to cause a snapping sound. With a curse Johnson fell in a crumpled mass.

Nausea was welling up in Marc's stomach from the blows and booze. He had to finish this quickly, before he passed out. So, he now moved to the thrown man who was picking himself up. With both hands clasped together Marc came down on the mans neck with all the limited force he had to muster. The man was smashed back to the ground without so much as a whimper.

Marc now forced himself to Rollies assistance. Rollie was being pounded by a series of kicks, for which his big frame was an easy target with little defense. Marc spun in a 360 turn with the ball of his foot smashing into McAdams with one hundred and eighty five pounds of torqued power. McAdams smashed against the porch, but to Marc's surprise he came back at Marc with a vengeance! His foot jab came with full force straight at Marc's chest. Marc moved his upper torso 90 degrees to the right, thus avoiding the kick. He grasped the leg with his right arm, and drove his left fist into the thigh muscle, causing considerable anguish. McAdams collapsed to the ground holding his leg, and cursing Trembley with vile language.

They were all now incapacitated.

Marc warned them all that if they try to come after him again, they would be dead meat, period.

Marc collected the dazed Rollie, and they left.

Chapter 12

The Enemy Within

Marc had Rollie follow him to a layby off nearby Interstate 76 so that he could park his big rig, and they could talk. Marc now knew he was against professionals and didn't want an innocent to get hurt. He had a hard time convincing Rollie that his services were not needed. Rollie thought that he could be of some help to Marc, especially with the intensity of the "combat" they had just encountered! Marc had a hard time convincing his friend that he could (now that he knew whom he was facing) take care of any eventualities. Marc prevailed when he told Rollie that weapons might be used, but only if absolutely necessary.

Marc had a good bottle of Chivas Regal in the car which he kept for special occasions. He broke it open so they could celebrate their friendship(and Rollie's departure)! Marc poured the prime whiskey into plastic cups and they drank to the little girls health, and to her mothers as well. Rollie knew there was something between Marc and the beautiful mother, but he said nothing. The two good friends finished their drinks, shook hands, and wished each other the best. Then Rollie reluctantly left.

Special Forces Captain Marc Trembley knew what the task was that lay before him, and he would implement that task with a vengeance! Marc drove back to his apartment. He went directly to an old locked briefcase. He took out a worn journal. The journal was marked "Top Secret", but had a mark across the category with some initials and a further classification of "Declassified". Marc studied lists, codes, and names amid a maze of information contained in the document. This was in fact a CIA dossier. Marc studied this journal of CIA information for two hours, but then he rose with a plan of action formulated in his keen mind.

To relax Marc did some warm up Chi Kung Exercises, a little Budo followed by T'ai Chi and meditation. It was an hour well spent for it relaxed both his body and his mind.

A cloudy chapter as a Central American field rep. was being recalled as he opened some long closed files. Marc made several calls with file in hand. The calls were short and concise. A series of events must now take place. He had now set up an unstoppable series of events that must come to a conclusion for better or worse! But this series of events would be on Marc's terms! He was now an unknown card in a deck of wild cards.

Marc still had a need for exercise, for anticipation had made him just a bit jumpy. For the next three hours the man in room 313 was just a dark silhouette of smooth moves and counter moves, finishing with the deadly art of Budo.

Marc showered, and then dressed in a conservative business suit that had a slight bulge over the heart. His black shoes were metal tipped, but light and flexible. Marc rounded up all his armor, and other necessities, and left.

He "cleansed" the room of any references to him, the CIA, or of the martial arts.

He now made two more calls, one to the local Porsche garage, and the other to a Yellow Cab Taxi.

The yellow cab took it's passenger to the main depot in the city, and it's passenger got on the first train.

The man with steel rimmed glasses was frowning, and his deep set eyes were riveted directly on Major John Robello with ferocious intensity. "All right explain it all from the beginning, and leave absolutely nothing out," exhaled the Assistant Director! The time has come to conclude our selections. and get on with #943 with post haste. "The floor is yours Major Robello, get on with it!"

Robello's face wag red, his eyes hard, and his jaw set. The story began to enfold in all it's graphic and violent detail. A few personal details were left out(for self preservation's sake).

The other two men in the room didn't look too happy either, for their turn was yet to come!

The A. D. continued, "do you "black belts" need help in a simple "neutralization?" Why is this man so hard to handle?"

Johnson answered with disbelief of what had happened still in his voice. I thought we had him pretty well set up, but he is very good.

The A. D. was incredulous, "then it's true that he was drunk and you couldn't take him!"

"Well Robello, do you need more expert help? What about Kim, he's ninth or tenth degree, isn't he?"

John Robello was not happy to be the messenger of the A. D., or anyone else! Particularly if it was a caper that any fool could do. Any lower order operative well down in the echelon could check out an old code and unused rendezvous. This rendezvous was a little used phone booth on a mariner's dock.

Assignments were set, so Robello drove to the dock. The marina was dark and quiet after the days activities. A few lights from a yacht in the harbor and two fishing boats at the dock were the only things visible through the pitch blackness.

The Major cut out the engine on his big Grand Prix and opened his glove compartment door. I must be getting senile he thought my automatic must still be in my desk drawer. Oh well! He thought it's probably nothing anyway, my thirty eight special will do!

As he left his car, he picked up his flashlight, then proceeded toward the phone booth. He didn't quite make it. The darkness exploded in a blaze of light in his face, there was pain, and then nothing.

He was out for a long time. It was damp and cold as the bloodshot eyes of the disheveled Major tried to open. He tried to get to his feet, but to no avail! He was still very groggy, but from what he didn't know! His mind wouldn't function, and his body was very, very heavy. it took Robello about ten minutes to recover enough to even start the thinking process.

What had happened, and who had done this to him?

His neck hurt like hell, and his eyes smarted, but otherwise he had survived the ordeal!

He felt for his thirty eight, but it was missing! Damn it he must have lost it when he was hit. His wallet was also gone! He had just been mugged, and he didn't know by whom!

His keys were gone as well. He looked for the Grand Prix, but it had been stolen as well.

He had no choice but to bum a ride! It was a bedraggled and forlorn agent who had to hike to the nearest highway looking for a ride back to civilization! Revenge was squarely on Major John Robello's mind, but on whom he still didn't know!

Captain Mark Trembley, former CIA Agent #321 knew only too well that his plan was working! His first step in letting the intelligence community know that "it" was being stalked had been completed. Robello was the first to know that it was an expert predator on the prowl.

Chapter 13

Counter Attack

The main railroad station was filled with holiday travelers as a businessman thumbed through the big city phone book. The atmosphere was noisy and congested, but ideal for the task that had to be done! The man's first call was to an old, but much used number. It had been changed as the man knew it would be! With a special code fed into the phone in an exact sequence the new number was given by a mechanical like voice on a tape recorder. The correct number also had another message, "The office is closed for repairs by the Sidney Magnalini Company", period.

The businessman took a very small recorder and a paperback book out of his pocket, and carefully placed them by the telephone receiver(with the recorder inside the paperback). He then retreated to a bench against the far wall, and sat down. He then began to read the "Times."

In about fifteen minutes, two big men in cheap looking blue business suits converged on the open receiver, one from the left and one from the right.

They seemed visibly upset that no one was at the phone to greet them! They seemed a little nervous and were still looking around for someone when they noticed the paperback book near the phone in the corner. There was something in the paperback. They looked at the apparatus with some consternation and some apprehension!

Suddenly there was a tremendous explosion. The blast knocked both men to the floor. They were knocked unconscious by the blast, tattered and torn, but alive!

Panic ensued throughout the whole area, and confusion as to what exactly had happened! The railroad station had marble floors and walls so that no fire followed the explosion, but smoke from the blast quickly filled the immediate area. People were running away from the blast area, some screaming and some cursing!

The man seated with the "Times" coolly got up and went over to the injured men. He noted that most people indeed were running away from the area of the explosion, even as he proceeded to search the two unconscious men. With quick deft moves he proceeded to extract their standard issue firearms and wallets. He opened his briefcase, and placed the items inside. The businessman now put his "Times" inside the briefcase, got up, and casually walked away. He vanished into the crowd leaving the area of the blast.

Within a few minutes the police arrived. They were followed by the Bomb Squad. The police were led by Detective John Riley of the Terrorist Unit.

Riley, a Lieutenant of Detectives surveyed the chaotic scene for any sign of the perpetrator, or perpetrators. None could be seen, as far as a cursory look of the bomb scene could reveal. He now looked to help the two injured men. They were alive and conscious, but very bloody and groggy. He helped the injured men to a waiting ambulance. He would interrogate them later at the hospital, but first he must find the culprit or culprits of this unusual bombing!

Surveying the smoky scene Riley noticed something peculiar. In the middle of the debris the Lieutenant of Detectives saw an incredible sight. Lying clean and untouched by the explosion in the middle of the spectacle was a clean white envelope with typing on it! It was addressed to "The Chief of Detectives". Riley picked it up with slight suspicion that it might be another bomb. The note inside read, "These men are CIA Operatives from Langley, their immediate boss is Major John Robello, and his superior is Assistant Director Goodwin Hatfield." The note continued, "Their illegal firearms and identification have been confiscated for the public good."

Detective Lieutenant John Riley was confused. Why would anyone identify these men or their superiors? Why were they not killed instead of this humiliation and identification?

Riley was aroused from his confused state of mind by a strong hand on his shoulder. "What to hell's going on," exclaimed Captain Eckert. Has anyone been killed?

Riley said, "no to both questions" answering to his superior in the Detective Branch! Riley continued to say that he had found this envelope with the odd note inside! He handed both pieces of evidence to Eckert.

Eckert thought that it might be a joke, especially as he could not think of who would do this to the CIA! He would have to check it out with this Robello and Hatfield just in case it wasn't a joke.

This was all very unusual. It was definitely not to these two veteran city cops liking, not at all! The questions kept coming back to him. Were they truly CIA men? Why would someone rob them of their weapons and identification? Why were they not killed by the bomb? There was more than meets the eye here, and that at least was a certainty!

Chapter 14

Other Worries

Judy was happy to be free of any other responsibility, or even affection, in her all too busy life. Raising her Allicin, and keeping food on the table was enough to worry about, for the time being!

Marc Trembley was a sad chapter in her life that must be forgotten. The question that remained was, could she learn to forget the man that she had come to love? The problem was not only emotional entanglement, but his protection and friendship to both her and Allicin! As a matter of fact she had just moved after considering Marc's suggestion to do so! Even if no trouble from her association with Marc came, bad memories would still remain.

The duplex she moved to had a nice young couple with two adopted kids living with them. The husband worked for the government, but was home on a regular basis(she noticed). This made Judy feel a bit easier, just having some kind of man around. The husband wasn't a Marc Trembley, but at least he was big, and drove a black Trans-Am! Judy laughed to herself for her own little joke.

In the middle of her laugh, the doorbell rang. A well dressed oriental man was smiling through the door at her. The man seemed somewhat familiar, but he had seen her in any case, so she answered the door.

"I am Young Kuo Kim, and I believe that we met in that bad bar room", volunteered the sanguine Mr. Kim.

"That is correct said the cautious Judy" remembering the man's catlike quickness.

As you may remember, I assisted Mr. Trembley in the trouble which unfortunately engulfed us all! I am now looking to assist him in some potential trouble that is close at hand.

"What a strange way of putting close at hand, in conjunction with, some potential trouble", Judy mused!

"Could you tell me please where Mr. Trembley may be?" Continued Kim with the interrogation. *I must find him to help him, no?*

"That was it" thought Judy, "No! I have no idea where Mr. Trembley is." continued the worried Judy. *He is such a violent man, so we had to split up.*

I am sorry to hear this, was the response. *Could you give him a message if you see him?* "I hope not to see him, but I will tell him if I ever do see him," answered Judy.

"Thank you, You are most kind," remarked Kim in his closing reply!

The Korean smiled, bowed, and abruptly left.

Judy watched the oriental leave the house, but he didn't leave the area! He sat in a parked sports car for a half hour, and then he left. But, had he left? Judy couldn't be sure! For all that pleasant facade presented to her, Judy was a bit scared of this man. The deadly and decisive way he had acted in the bar made Judy wonder, "could Marc counter such a man?"

Whether he was friend or foe Judy must let Marc know that the oriental was on his trail. Perhaps she could leave a message with Mrs. Vincinto! This she would do.

Judy's call to Mrs. Vincinto at the boarding house did little to settle her apprehension. Kim had visited her, and Marc was not at home. He would be away for a few days.

She now remembered how his controlled anger had scared her, and she had worried what this violent man she loved might do! Then there was the story going around the campus about Josh Logan's "come uppance"! She was now sure of one thing, Captain Marc Trembley of the Special Forces was now on the attack! And heaven help the people he was after!

The question now arose, "was it safe in this city, or even the state for her and Allicin?" Marc's associates and adversaries could be anywhere! These answer-less questions were troubling indeed!

She could not in good conscience turn her whole life around on the supposition that trouble is, or is not brewing! Besides, I have God and Marc Trembley on my side she thought! The problem with that thought was, she had separated from Marc. It seemed that this short relationship was almost like marriage separation How strange life was! Furthermore it also seemed that life was dangerous without him, as well as with him!

Perhaps she thought she should let the man next door know she would appreciate his observance of any auspicious people nosing about? She must not alarm him, just keep him alert to possible danger.

"Possibly I should alert the police as well," she mused! Certainly they would understand, and offer some advice.

Her decisions were made. Judy then called the police. The local police couldn't get involved, as no crime had been committed. Judy stressed the fact that she had been attacked before, and that the police had not caught the attacker. They said that they were sorry, but that they didn't have cause to protect her.

This elegant little lady was now ripping mad that the law officials couldn't, or wouldn't get involved! "What must I do to get you involved, get murdered?" She yelled this at the inanimate object, just as she smashed it onto it's receiver!

With the exasperating call to the police over with, Judy now turned her focus to her next door neighbor.

The man next door was Jonathan Quigley. Quigley worked for the government in Virginia. He was a big man physically who enjoyed sports and chess, but not interruptions! He had come home early to get some of the inexhaustible paperwork that seemed to proliferate when adverse news was received at the office. The third dossier was the real pain, and he was stumped on how to approach the problem. He was interrupted from this infernal problem by the infernal doorbells noisy ringing.

Irritably he went to the door. Standing in his alcove was none other than his new neighbor, and a pretty one at that!

After mutual introductions were over Quigley invited Judy in for the chat that she wanted.

He seemed more amused than surprised when he heard her tale of woe and apprehension! None the less Judy received assurances that if he was needed he would help.

He thought that he would offer Judy a coffee to settle her obviously frayed nerves, but she declined.

As she got up to leave Judy noticed that Quigley's open briefcase had a leather belt with a leather attachment to it mixed among the manila folders. "He's a bit odd keeping his belt in his briefcase," thought the amused Judy!

"To each his own", said Judy to herself.

Judy's mind was now in less of a turmoil with the thought that at least someone else was aware of her situation. His size alone might frighten people! With this in mind Judy returned to her new abode to continue preparing it for living.

What Mrs. Vincinto didn't tell Judy was the circumstances of Kim's visit. In fact Kim was waiting for Marc in his room. He was calmly seated in a chair by the window.

"Good morning," he said. "Could you tell me where Mr. Trembley has gone?"

In the middle of the room was her coffee table, and it was split into two shattered pieces of polished hardwood.

What Mrs. Vincinto didn't know was that Kim Sou Dong the Korean National Karate Champion in a fit of rage(that his quarry had flown the nest) had exploded with a karate chop that severed her table!

Mrs. Vincinto was not usually a woman who scared easily, but this man was different in some sinister way. His eyes seemed to look straight through her mind! His calm exterior exude a kind of ferocious concentration that was readily apparent. Here was a man not to be crossed. The not so-subtle questions that she wanted to ask this man were stymied in their stride.

"I am Kim, a friend of Mr. Trembley's," was the quick response to the situation. You have my deepest apologies for my clumsy actions in your very pleasant home. Of course I will pay you recompense for the accidental destruction of your lovely table! As Kim spoke he handed Mrs. Vincinto three crisp one hundred dollar bills.

She was amazed at the gesture! She just didn't quite know what to expect.

Kim bowed, and then gracefully left the room. It was almost like a panther slinking away after his kill.

Gloria Vincinto turned to pick up the pieces of her fractured table, but was surprised to hear Kim Sou Dong's voice from the doorway!

"Did Mr. Trembley indicate where he was going, or whom he was going to see," asked the shrewd Mr. Kim(hoping to catch her off balance)?

"Mr. Trembley's life is very quiet, and I don't know where he is she lied." This was the comment offered by Gloria Vincinto to this mercurial oriental!

"His girl friend is recovering nicely in the hospital," offered Mr. Kim.

This latest interrogation(and that it was) did not catch her by surprise this time.

Her answer set Mr. Kim into consternation, yet his resolve became quite apparent in his expression. Kim was enraged that this mere landlady was offering resistance to an expert interrogator!

Kim knew that an offer of money for information would not settle well with this tough closed mouthed woman. He also knew that force would be counter productive as well. Having been beaten at his own game, he smiled, bowed, and left without another word.

It just didn't seem right to Gloria Vincinto, and she made a mental note to tell the nice Mr. Trembley all about Mr. Kim's actions.

Chapter 15

A Terrorist Act

The Virginia evening was sweet and cool among the mangroves near the two fine Georgian buildings. The main building was kept in the finest of southern traditions with formal gardens and long stretches of green lawn. It sat on one hundred and twenty acres of gently rolling hills. A perfect scene of tranquillity. The other smaller building housed the few servants quarters and guest rooms.

This was not the house of a "normal" government servant. It was in fact the home of the powerful Assistant Director, CIA.

The AD'S Watch, it was called by the agents who got this "plum". It was usually uneventful and awfully boring, but a nice change from the "Operations Side" of the dice! The agents sat in two cars. One was at the metal gate at the entrance. The other was discretely parked at the side of the main house.

Dean Hargraves was a new CIA Agent, and a recent graduate of the "Academy". The reason he had joined was for excitement, but that didn't appear to be on his immediate horizon. Being a baby sitter for the AD was not exactly a life threatening situation! The cool Virginia evening was quiet, quiet as the dead.

Hargraves partner who was sitting by the front gate in the baby sitting assignment was an old timer. George Plotkin. Plotkin was getting ready to retire, and conversely didn't mind this easy duty. It was a beautiful Virginia evening, and he loved the quiet.

Goodwin Hatfield had just finished bidding good night to the last member of The Committee On Terrorism when the feeling came! The AD felt clammy and the *hair on the back of his neck prickled in an ominous omen. Being a prudent and very practical man he would usually dismiss this as ridiculous, but he was soon to be alone! His wife Janet was at her mothers, and the servants were off for the night as well. He had dismissed the servants for the night to assure absolute confidentiality for the committee. It was just a passing phase he thought, and besides their were two agents on the premises. With these thoughts he dismissed the bad omens.*

The work was piling up, especially with the Congress getting interested in his responsibility of Covert Operations.

He decided to call his Personal Secretary June Kilgore over to see if they could flatten the pile of paperwork he had taken home. When he tried the phone it was dead! A second "secure" line was in the back bedroom. Hatfield was not a man to scare easily, but he was concerned as he went to the bedroom. He knew that he was in trouble as soon as he entered the bedroom. The ominous feelings and forebodings returned.

A powerful arm seized his neck in a vise like hold. Simultaneously, a hand holding chloroform covered his nose and mouth. But Hatfield was no ordinary AD! He had come up from the ranks as a top agent(no appointee this man). He had just enough time to get off a backward jab with an elbow into Marc Trembley's side. It was too little and too late, the chloroform took hold! Hatfield was out cold on the floor in seconds. Marc trussed him together arms to legs in an irregular curve backwards. Marc rose with Goodwin Hatfield on his shoulders. It was only then that he realized that Hatfield's desperate elbow thrust had caught him. Driven by fear and adrenaline this paper pusher had done what professional assassins had failed to do. As Marc straightened his legs with Hatfield on his shoulders excruciating pain emanated from his side. Marc felt nausea in his stomach, and then he felt blood on his side. As he looked at his bloody side Marc saw something on the floor. On the rug beside Hatfield's big desk he saw his folly. A light from the adjoining den glinted on the sharp and bloodied big ornamental letter opener(shaped like a dagger) on the floor beside the desk. On his desperate attempt to dislodge the iron grip on his neck Hatfield's elbow had thrust the implement into Marc's side!

Marc knew that he must get back to his car before his strength waned from the loss of blood. As he left the house luck was with him as clouds overshadowed the moon. Marc's familiarity with CIA procedures and surveillance techniques had come in handy with this "caper". He knew the shift change routine gave him about ten minutes to carry out his acquisition!"

The two men at the side of the house were too busy talking to notice the shadowy exit from the rear of the house. Marc had parked his car in some trees well away from the house on a dirt road. Marc dumped the limp body into his cars trunk, locked it, then drove away without incident.

The plan was firm in mind, and it only required "normal" procedure on everyone's part in order for it to work.

The bleeding was an unforeseen, and would require immediate attention. He must be prepared for more trouble as he was facing professionals and not a klutz like Hogan! Judy was the only one Marc could trust for such a delicate task. He was sorry to think of her further implication, but it was an absolute necessity.

Marc had special plans for Mr. Goodwin Hatfield, plus a lot of people in the intelligence community. Done right this could be fun, or it could be the final act in this "Wisdom Seeker's" life! The truth of the matter that Marc had to admit to himself was, "vengeance was going to be sweet".

Marc drove for two hours, and arrived at his retreat in worsening shape. He was glad he had given Hatfield a "shot" as he didn't know if he could handle a squirming body! Marc had taken a pep pill(not his custom, but helpful this time) to keep himself going. The ongoing arrangements he had made were already in place, and Hatfield would be taken care of. Two old friends from the past greeted him at the retreat, and took Hatfield off his hands. They would be kept anonymous, as he wished Judy could have been!

Unfortunately, she would be "in harms way" for a short while.

Now he must take care of his wound, which was bleeding through his makeshift bandage, and making him a bit dizzy.

Marc stopped at a bar to make the call to Mrs. Vincinto, and have her get in touch with Judy.

Mrs. Vincinto explained about the Korean gentleman who was looking for him, and how he had broken her lovely table!

So Kim was on my trail he mused, I must get ready. The question was how to divert Kim? He must get some medical help, or Kim would demolish him in his present shape!

On the other hand most things would lead any good agent to him, eventually. Marc would have Mrs. Vincinto and Judy lead Kim to the wrong place!

Marc would then have time to get some medical help before he became useless to himself, or anyone else!

Marc would then contact an outpatient clinic to get some medical help. The cut in his side might have come from any sharp instrument, and not necessarily a knife!

"What is the smallest private clinic or hospital outside the city," Marc asked the indomitable Mrs. Vincinto? She thought for a minute and then responded with the necessary information. "I'll call the Daniel Moran Hospital in suburban Peabody, "she said. "It's not well known, but it has a good reputation."

"Would you please call Judy, and ask for her to wait for me there?"

"Certainly Mr. Trembley, but are you all right?" came the follow up question from the worried Mrs. V.

The city run outpatient clinic Marc actually went to was located on a side street opposite the cities high school. It was a blackboard jungle encased in red brick, and was reminiscent of a mill town.

Marc had bought a bottle of cheap whiskey, drank a bit and spilled some on his shirt. So, it was a scruffy destitute alcoholic who arrived at the clinic. He was hurt foraging through a dumpster for half empty bottles.

Nurse Sandra Deane did not really believe this big and good looking man for a minute! First, he was too well groomed under the superficial dirt and messed up clothing. Secondly, he was not emaciated!

Thirdly, he wore expensive sneakers, which were relatively new! Fourth and most important for a nurse, he had the well tuned body of an athlete!

"Follow me," said Nurse Deane. Marc followed the nurse to a small examination room at the rear of the clinic.

Chapter 16

Controls Help

"Strip to the waist," came the order from Mz. Sandra Deane. She proceeded to examine the wound. It was obviously a knife wound, but it hadn't penetrated any major arteries or organs. Sandra cleaned and dressed the wound. The covering bandages were extensive, and relatively tight.

Ms. Sandra Deane told Mr. John Smith to lie down for an hour to see if the bleeding would stop.

Marc welcomed the chance to rest, and to think his plans through!

Sandra Deane on the other hand welcomed the chance to call the police, and to have this well conditioned "alcoholic" checked out! She called her friend in the police department to do just that! Hello! I would like to talk with Sergeant Bill Rankel please! Rankel came on the line.

"Hello Sandra, it's a long time since I heard this pretty voice!" What can I do for you?

"I have an outpatient you might be interested in, because he's different!"

"In what way, "continued Rankel ?

When Sandra explained, something clicked with Rankel.

"I'll be over in a short while!"

Marc's throat was dry so he got up for a drink of water. That's when he noticed Nurse Deane on the pay phone near the front door. Now, why wouldn't she use the phone at her desk? It just didn't fit. She must be calling the police! She had her back to Marc so he slipped quietly out the rear door.

As he was set to drive away from his parking spot in front of the school, he noticed the unmarked car coming slowly toward him. It was obviously a police car with the one neutral color, two antennas, and the city number plate. It was almost laughable, but they were after him! There were two plain clothes policeman in the front seat, with two uniformed officers in the back seat. Marc would let them pass before he would make his move to safety. The car pulled up to the clinic. They stopped, and three policemen went through the front door.

Marc made his move. He backed the Porsche out of the one way street without incident! He drove back to his apartment in a very tired state. His body needed rest, but he had some calls to make first.

His first call was to Judy. Judy was surprised enough with the instructions from Mrs. Vincinto, but even more when Marc wasn't at the suburban hospital described in the phone conversation! She had just returned when Marc called. She was mad and relieved, and all at the same time! She had missed Marc more than she would admit to herself(until now). She was glad that he was not dead or something. But, why the charade? Why the phone call? Why have her go to the dammed hospital in the first place?

Marc explained that he had to divert his adversaries for a while to gain time.

"Are you hurt," Judy inquired?

"Just a minor cut that is now taken care of," he explained.

"It seems that we can't live with, or without each other," said Judy wistfully!

"What is the next move?"

"Were you followed to the hospital? Did you see any suspicious men sitting in the waiting room," Marc continued asking? "If there was you would have led them a merry chase. Right?"

Judy didn't answer. She just shook her head in agreement. She didn't know if this was a dangerous game, or what!

Chapter 17

A Maize / A Gauntlet

The Director was a man of enormous integrity, but with the same amount of impatience to match it as well! His second in command was not around to answer to certain peculiarities that the director had accidentally discovered. He needed more information, and to get this information he needed his AD Goodwin Hatfield. He knew that Goodwin's somewhat unorthodox schedule was such that he wouldn't be available for ten(count them) days!

Perhaps Goodwin's Secretary June Kilgore could shed some light on this matter of covert operations in Central America?

The Director turned to his secretary Delores. Delores could you check with June and see if Goodwin left any typing for the Committee on Terrorism? The Director's verbal eruption was loud and spontaneous. He had important meetings coming up, and he must get the facts, and have them at his fingertips.

Delores returned from Hatfield's office after first checking in June's office, but found nothing on the subject.

"I'm sorry sir, but I found nothing on either desk on that subject," Delores exclaimed! They are both out of the office this week. The AD is away on several security meetings. June is on vacation as agreed!

"What do you mean as agreed," demanded Alfred Whittier Greenfield?

Delores explained, that with national security in mind, they had agreed that June would take her vacation when he was away at meetings.

"Sensible, but who minds the store," exclaimed the Director in dismay?

"You do Sir."

Major Robello and Robertson are your expert consultants for these periods.

"Good, contact both of them, and tell them that I need to review The Committee on Terrorism's progress immediately! No excuses are to be accepted from either man period."

"Understand?"

"Yes Sir?"

"I don't usually get into operations, but it seems I will have to! "I will get to the bottom of this puzzle," exclaimed the Director!

"Delores cancel all my appointments for this afternoon. I will meet with the majors in one hour. Order a very strong pot of coffee and sandwiches to be sent to my office as well!"

Delores knew it was serious when the Director ordered very strong coffee.

At precisely 2:00 PM both men arrived with bulging briefcases, and possibly trepidation in their hearts.

Robertson was the first to enter. As he entered he glanced at Greenfelds "in" basket, and noticed that his registered letter was still unopened. He then looked at a thoroughly enraged Robello who didn't look the best for wear physically, or mentally! The man seemed ready to crack. Then he did crack! To Robertson's surprise an awkward but powerful "jordan" Handblade move emanated from the thoroughly exasperated Robello! In a quick smoothly flowing motion Robertson's right hand closed over the back of Robello's wrist. He employed Robello's momentum, leverage, and the "pendulum principle" to forcibly seat the amazed Robello!

To say the least Greenfeld was completely taken aback!

Robello was humiliated and completely defeated by Robertson's quick Akido move. It was doubly demeaning in front of the Director.

Grenfeld didn't usually allow the pleasant release of his pent up anger. This time he did. "God dam it what to hell is the matter with you two guys?" "Control youselves," he continued! "These aren't the jungles of Central America, and there not the streets of Lebanon." "Cool it!" While you do that I'll check some important mail.

Robello now became more enraged, but he just managed to control himself by adjusting his disarranged shirt and tie.

Robertson on the other hand simply eased out of his "jigota(an Akido stance)" to an military at ease stance. it was as if nothing had happened!

The Director now spoke to his subordinates in his authoritative tone of command. "Impressive Major Robertson, but relatively easy for the Agencies Chief Authority on Martial Arts!"

The two men were silent as the Director examined his curiously large pile of mail. The registered letter from Richardson was near the top, but unopened.

The other letter of explanation from Marc was just below Major Richardson's letter(Delores always put the registered letters together). The small package with Robello's gun was opened by Langley's security people upon receipt that very morning. The enclosed note read, "This pistol and I. D. belong to Major John Robello. They are standard Agency issue."

The letter from Trembley explained Robello's, The AD's, Johnson's, Ander's and McAdam's roles in Tremble's demise. Marc also explained his position on File #1701. Marc's call to his "Control(Robertson)" in Central America was coming to fruition as well.

Greenfeld read Marc's letter a second time. The significance began to sink in! Security had sent him the envelope, with the gun and badge in earlier that morning. He now placed this envelope containing the hardware into his top drawer. Now the inquisition would begin in earnest! With a set expression on his face he began the questioning.

"Mr. Robello, where is Your Pistol and ID?"

"I lost them Sir," exclaimed the confused Major John Robello!"

"What were the circumstances?" continued the Director.

Robello was forced to reiterate the situation as it happened.

"Why are excessive surveillance hours put on a former agent, and one with an excellent record?"

"Why did your personal hardware, and that of two of your agents turn up at Langley?"

"It seams that Mr. Marc Trembley has made his case. it is also quite apparent that he is still the very best."

"If he had gone to the other side Mr. Robello(when the Director was mad he used last names and not titles) wouldn't Trembley have killed or captured your two agents?"

"For that matter he could have killed you at will!"

"Why were you doing this to Captain Trembley?"

"He was one of the final two candidates for The Committee on Terrorism's Object Team." The answer didn't satisfy the Director.

"Was the other candidate harassed, attacked and followed as Trembley was?"

"No Sir."

"Was the other candidate as good as Trembley?"

"Yes Sir!"

"Not so," said Robertson curtly, his voice cutting into their conversation!

"What is it Robertson demanded the furious Director?"

"I trained both men, and Trembley's the best I've seen in Years. And we know who is the smartest, don't we!"

"The director continued the interrogation. I would like to tidy up some loose ends Mr. Robello."

"The Korean national you hired, where is he, and what assignment did you give him?" The inquisitor continued.

Robello knew that the only way to save his neck was to come clean and tell all he knew. "If I tell you all of the plan will you absolve me?"

I will absolve you on two conditions. "One is that you resign from the agency. Two is that you meet Trembley and apologize, or meet him in a gym, and settle this man to man without the use of weapons.

"I have information on the AD, and I will act on it personally."

Robello's face turned ashen, even as he recognized his new predicaments extent.

Robertson had a slight smile on his face, as the Director continued.

"Again, what is Kim's task?" he asked.

Robello hesitated, but Robertson was about to extract the information the hard way, so he continued. He told Greenfeld the information in a slow whisper.

"Too wipe out Trembley in any way that he can."

Robertson became the inquisitor. "Does Kim have help?"

"Yes."

"How many?"

"Two, "came the answer.

"Are they both armed?"

"Yes."

"Where is the ambush to take place?"

"Where ever or when ever Trembley is alone."

Chapter 18

The Showdown

Marc had just made all the calls, and all the arrangements were in place. He knew that he must get some rest, and then select the arena for the first yet final meeting with Kim.

Marc's body was now weary, and he grabbed his outside mirror for leverage, and knocked something to the ground. It was a microphone. He was "made!" He reached down to pick it up. Marc heard the light step of a possible assailant directly behind him. Instead of straightening up Marc threw himself on the ground. The garrote of Mosha Hadike sliced through the air in only a harmless preparation for death! As Marc turned toward his assailant his legs caught his attackers leading leg in a powerful scissors action, thus throwing the attacker off balance. Marc rose quickly to a crouch. The attacker kicked hard at Marc's head. Marc performed a "ward off left" action driving the mans leg up and over his shoulder. Marc now drove his fist in a corkscrew motion into the mans groin. He rose with the punch giving it the additional power of his body behind it! The assailant screamed, and then passed out. He laid on his back as peaceful as a baby in a crib.

Marc didn't wait to find out who his assailant was! He collected his thoughts and tired body, and drove away.

Funny thing Marc kept on thinking, he had deadly intent, but it wasn't a problem!

"Was Kim trying to wear him down before their showdown ?"

"Or was it one of his other enemies?"

"He just didn't know!"

Someone, probably Kim or Robello knew every move that he made! Marc could use this to advantage, and he would! "I will meet you for a formal showdown at the local YMCA, in two days" he announced.

Marc then drove to the nearest hotel, and proceeded to sleep for ten hours. His ten hours was only broken alternately practicing T'ai-Chi-Chaun, Ti-Quan-Do, Akido, and Budo. The next day was the same, sleep and practice. Marc became thoroughly rested, and "tuned" like a powerful well oiled machine.

At 5:00 he called Judy at her duplex, directly, therefore ensuring the enemy would know the arrangements. Now the final act could be played.

Judy was worried because Rollie, Robello, Robertson, and the police had been in touch with her and looking for Marc.

He must show the Intelligence Community that he will not, and more importantly, would not be intimidated, or coerced!

Marc made one more call. The call would be received by Robello and Co., and would ensure the safety of Marc and all his friends.

The handball court that Marc had already reserved would be ideal for this "Martial Arts Confrontation." Marc arrived at exactly 4:45 PM. He had to park about two miles away from the gym. This was to be expected, at an inner city gym on Saturday. The YMCA was relatively crowded.

Marc went up to the reservations desk too check in. He inquired of the reservation of the clerk.

"A Mr. Kim, your handball opponent is waiting for you at court nine," the attendant told Marc.

"Thank you."

When Marc signed the register the attendant remarked on Marc's wrist straps.

"Why do you wear these straps?"

A truthful answer came back from Marc. "For power!"

The man was silent.

Marc went to handball court #9. As he entered the court two men on either side of the court started to approach Marc.

"NO!" Came a command from center court.

"Both of you get out!" This was their last command. They left the court.

Marc was not unhappy to see them leave, for one Korean Master would be enough too handle!

One man now stood at center court.

Kim Si Dong was a sight to behold! His Tae-Kwon-Do robes were of black silk with a multi-colored dragon with two heads glaring out at Marc. His headband was pure white. as was his wristbands. His feet were bare. This indicated that the ball of the foot, the heel, and the foot-sword were hardened weapons.

This ever so polite Asian asked Marc, "would Mr. Trembley like to warm up before we begin?"

"Has Mr. Kim completed his warm up?" Marc countered!

"You are very kind," came Kim's reply.

The individual assessments by each of the other would now commence.

Kim commenced with breathing and squatting exercises, nothing else! He then settled into meditation.

Marc went into a light warm-up consisting of Animal Frolics and Brocades. Marc would soon find out if he was to get a full attack, or a measured response Kim suddenly straightened up from his meditation and announced that "we shall begin!"

The two combatants circled each other like two tigers circling for the kill. Their soft and lithe steps belied the deadly potential energy that was waiting to be expended.

Mark struck first using a single knuckle punch to the base of ribs. It was meant as a parry.

Kim blocked it down and away, with a quick left hand-sword blow to Marc's forearm. Simultaneously, Kim's right hand shot out with fingers extended toward Marc's wound.

Marc turned on the balls of his feet in the direction the hand-blade had forced his arm too go. He stepped backward with his right foot. He then entangled Kim's left arm in a scissors action. The momentum carried Kim forward.

Kim was folded up, and his weight brought forward. Rotating without pause, Marc stepped to Kim's rear(again) with his right foot placing it behind Kim's left calf. The momentum had swept Kim downward, and then backward onto his back.

At the moment of impact Marc's sweeping right hand blade caught Kim on the temple.

The stunned Kim was still able to grab Marc's lower arm in a powerful wrist lock, which pulled Marc off balance. Marc rolled in the direction of the twisted arm to the floor.

Both men spun to their feet.

The protagonists commenced with a series of lightning parries and punches to the head, body, and arms of each other.

With the first strike over, the preliminaries had resumed!

Perhaps from the oriental's "inner space" exploded a powerful snap kick. It caught Mare's blocking arms with near deadly accuracy, and with numbing impact. The severity of the incredibly fast blow threw Marc against the wall. Marc's right arm was pounded numb, and was now badly bruised by the callused foot blade.

Kim sensed a fast kill, and hurtled his whole body behind a roundhouse kick at Marc's chest or head.

Marc withdrew his crossed hands, and sank his body into a rollback, and the inevitable T'ai Chi Push followed. The thrust and momentum of Kim was projected upward.

Marc's shoulders, back, trunk, and powerful legs hurtled Kim's body into a circular spinning arc. As Kim head spun back and upward from the aporge(low point), Marc made his final move. Marc's clasped hands come down from their perigee(high point) above his head. The swift bludgeon collided with Kim's neck. The devastating impact smashed Kim to the floor. The ultimate black belt lay in a grotesque heap on the handball floor.

The reverberation and power of the deadly collision left Marc empty, robbed, and exhausted. He was mentally and physically spent. He collapses beside the prostrate body of Kim.

Marc's dulled brain tried to remember the inner strengths he had garnered from T'ai Chi Chaun, Kempo, Okinowan, and the Budo Mystiques! He had used his inner energy(Chi or Qi), or the power of the mind to strengthen the body to defeat Kim. The Tai-Sabaki(turning movement) was used to turn the power of Kim into a dissipating circular movement. Where was his restraint? Why had he been maneuvered into his darker side? These questions bothered this seeker of wisdom!

The American victor was sitting in oriental repose, collecting mind and spirit when he noticed the tattoos on the prostrate figure. The opponent he had just defeated was not Kim! He couldn't believe it, but it was true! Kim had only one tattoo, on his right forearm, not multiples! Marc knew it well, it was a beautiful dragon that indicated a "black" society, or some mysterious Korean clan!

A soft, and faintly familiar voice drifted across the room and taunted the weary martial artist!

"A credible, but crude defense and attack Captain Marc Trembley," revealed the real Kim Si Dong!

Marc was stunned, and could hardly believe it. He had defeated the wrong man!

"How could he not have remembered that cool measured voice with the slight English accent?"

"How could he have forgotten that one glaring dragon?"

The fact was he had barely defeated the second team! His mind raced, and his supple body tensed. It was no consolation that his toughest enemy sat quietly composed opposite him, even as his own bruised and tired body tensed!

The "real" Kim continued, "we must define the discipline and rules to be used in our educational exercise!"

"Good God thought Marc, "he intends to show a Ninth Degree Black Belt, and Seventh Dan the finer points of self defense! "Incredible!"

The next utterance was even more incredible!

"We shall meet, but not this day!"

"You must be one hundred percent fit for me to defeat you", the master of the moment announced!

"My win must not be contaminated by a weak, or second rate, opponent!"

"You will call me when You are strictly one hundred percent fit, and not before", instructed the officious oriental! Having instructed the infidel in the rules of the same, Kim left the room.

Marc heard a commotion outside the room, and then there was absolute quiet! Marc got up and cautiously opened the door. Lying on the floor were three CIA

Agents who were out cold! They must have tried to take Kim or his impostor into custody. At Major Robertson's behest they must have tried to take the supposed killer of Marc Trembley into custody.

Robertson arrived, and seemed quite amused at the turn of events! The agents were roughed up, but more embarrassed than hurt.

"Did you defeat Kim, "Robertson asked Trembley?

"No, I didn't meet him," Marc responded!

"Who did you meet?"

"I don't know!"

"Did you defeat him?"

"Yes!"

Major Robertson, "Kim has done no wrong, so do not try to apprehend him!" Marc volunteered the information to diffuse the situation a bit!

"Was Kim part of Robello's little band of assassins," Major Robertson asked?

"I don't know, but I doubt it," was Marc's reply!

As the conversation continued, Marc took note of the loquacious man standing opposite him. An interesting man thought Marc. Robertson is of average height, average build, relatively good looking with no distinguishing marks. In point of fact he's the perfect agent. The perfect British Agent? The man's movement is as fluid as a meandering estuary softly gliding through the countryside. He exhibits absolutely no wasted actions or movement. What was he doing in the employ of the CIA? He would take some looking into, this Major Elliott Robertson, Sr. Agent, CIA!

Chapter 19

The Wisdom Seeker

When Marc confided in Robertson, a smile broke out on the man's stoic face. Marc was glad to leave the responsibility of Robello to Robertson. He knew there would inevitably be more questions, and these would be answered, but all in good time.

Robertson assured Marc that all the "teams" on his trail would be called in!

He also assured Marc that his "ace in the hole", the SBIAP Situation be checked out, and corrected.

Marc was now completely exhausted, and this was apparent to Robertson.

"Take. several days to rest up, and then come to me. In the meantime I will talk with the mercurial Mr. Kim. We can then talk of this situation in more detail."

Marc's face suddenly showed disdain, when he remembered the AD, Mr. Goodwin Hatfield!

"Is their another problem I can help you with?" asked the observant Robertson!

"As a matter of fact there is, but it's more yours than mine!"

"Really! And what might that be?"

Marc continued, "The Assistant Director is presently detained in a local institution. He is continually sedated, but is otherwise okay. He is the central character in this play of many acts!"

Robertson was amazed! He had been told that Goodwin Hatfield would be absent for a while, but he had assumed it was "company business"! It was always a vague reference that he got to Hatfield's absence. He also knew there was a bit of a cloud over the AD, but it was not his affair.

Robertson's thoughts came back to Marc Trembley, the ultimate warrior.

"The heights to which you have gone can only be exceeded by the possible depths to which you still could go, Mr. Marc Trembley, civilian!" Robertson's comment held some merit, but the drama was almost over!

As Captain Marc Trembley's "control" Robertson was secretly pleased to hear of Mr. Goodwin Hatfields demise! The ladders rungs were far less than they had been of late.

Ah! Yes! The first stone had been cast, and by another disbeliever, and not himself!

"As you say, Marc I will deal with the AD, as well as the rest!"

Marc's quizzical look displayed the amazement he shows at the depth of Robertson's knowledge of the overall situation! Yet, he hadn't acted on that information. Why? That was the sixty four thousand dollar question.

A resolute Robertson stepped forward, and shook Marc's hand.

"Thanks for enabling a final take down," was Robertson's finishing touch to the episode.

The two men parted without another word.

Marc went to the YMCA reception desk and phoned Judy with the good news. She was relieved, and delighted to be free of anxiety at last.

"We can now get back to normal," she thought! She didn't express this to Marc over the telephone.

"What about Mr. Kim?" Was Judy's next question to Marc.

"Have you met him? Have you resolved your differences?"

Although ambiguities remained Marc allayed Judy's latent fears with a few calming platitudes!

Marc continued his pacification of Judy's fears. "The inexactitudes with the agency are being taken care of and I am to meet with Kim to resolve any problems that might remain with him."

"A compound statement for a compound situation," Marc thought to himself.

They agreed to rendezvous at a fine restaurant that evening and discuss all the irritants in their lives.

Marc then returned to the venerable Mrs. Vincinto's abode, and her supposed castigation. But, to his surprise she was delighted to see him in one piece!

Evidently the "table episode" had scared her pretty badly!

"Silly boy", thought Mrs. V. as she examined Marc's face. "I am scared for you! Why would anyone bother an old woman like me?"

Marc was honestly touched by this dear old gal. He leaned over and kissed this "five foot nothing on a brick", on the cheek.

"Really Mr. Trembley you smell! Go right up stairs and shower," exclaimed Mrs. V.! "And remember to shave as well. You must have at least two days stubble on that square jaw of yours!"

Marc laughed, but then retreated to the stairs in dutifully fashion.

He did just as Mrs. V. had said, and with a smile on his face to boot!

The former Captain of Special Forces Blue Team meditated for an hour. He stood with arms raised, chest sunk low, with his elbows slightly bent, but his back and torso were perfectly straight. His head was as if held by a single silk thread, and his tongue rested at the top of his mouth. The elastic figure in black followed this textbook "beginning" with a very slow half hour of T'ai Chi Chuan Yin Style Long Form.

Following the solo Exercise Sequence Marc showered and dressed in a very conservative blue suit, with gray argyle socks to match. He left the boarding house to meet Judy at a "special" club.

As he exited the front door Marc glanced up and down the street. No black Trans-Am in sight!

A rejuvenated Marc practically skipped to his beautiful red sports car, and departed the premises without an "escort ".

The Conservative Club was an elite club owned by alumni of Judy's college. The club was swank, conformist, and definitely right of center.

The attendant at the door took Marc's keys with relative immunity to the red sports car's allure!

Admission was gained to the club by the following: A-The "right" name. B. The year of graduation as an alumnus. C. The "correct" sponsor or host. Marc's card, Captain Marc Trembley U. S. Army Special Forces worried the maitre-d! He was relieved and satisfied when Judy came to Marc's rescue. She submitted her parents name and 1956 graduation date to the computer search. The computers Genealogy Files confirmed that her mother and father had graduated in 1956. They also revealed that Judy had attended "the college", attained honor status, but had not finished.

This was all news to Marc.

While the "check" was going on Judy left Marc to go to their table as she had already been announced.

"Whom shall I say arrived," asked the maitre-d? Shall it be Mr. Trembley, Mr. Marc Trembley, or Captain Marc Trembley?

Marc's response was, "Captain R. Marc Trembley III ". A little fib never hurt anyone, especially a maitre-d of a snobbish "eatery"! The numbers three and one are close.

"Thank you sir," came the response of the maitre-d.

"Right this way Sir."

"Thank you" was Marc's polite response.

When Marc was ushered to Judy's table his heart skipped a beat! Judy was radiance itself. She wore a red silk blouse with a green pleated skirt. A small string of pearls hung around her soft neck. Her luxuriant hair hung in a loose ponytail that cascaded lightly down her silken back. She looked like a lovely young model.

Marc was overcome with admiration and desire. He leaned over and kissed her lightly on the lips.

Judy blushed slightly as Marc's hands loosely held her shoulders when he bent over to kiss her.

Marc sat down and ordered a bottle of his favorite Asti-Spumonti from the impatient waiter.

Judy began to chatter amiably about Allison, school, herself, and her part time job.

As Marc was listening to Judy's pleasant chatter, he suddenly remembered school! He had all but forgotten his first goal in life, in the midst all these troubled times! He must remake his life over to include university life again. Dean Anders must be the next person he sees, and very soon!

Judy continued to talk as she finished her lobster, and Marc his shrimp. This course was completed with a cognac and a coffee.

Marc told Judy-of his plans to go to Dean Anders and tell him what had happened. Marc would also tell him of his intention to continue at the university.

Judy agreed completely, but what of the Josh Logan types he might meet at the university, or elsewhere? He would invariably meet them!

Marc replied, "I'll cross those bridges when I get to them."

Why don't I take you home, Judy? I can do a crash course and try to catch up to the rest of the class!

"A good idea . . ." remarked Judy, I'll help organize the topics you should pursue.

"Let's go!"

The relaxed couple left the restaurant with a pleasant sense of purpose that was decidedly different from the recent past!

Back at Marc's apartment the two older students crammed, and crammed. Marc finally called it quits at eleven P. M.

Marc had made a mental reservation that he should keep their relationship as "pure" as possible for Allison's sake. But, this was becoming harder and harder to do!

Judy had borrowed a white T-shirt from Marc to save the new blouse from getting creased. The T-shirt was old, and had shrunk. Her lovely breasts pushed against the thin cotton. This revealed everything the shirt tried to contain.

Judy just laughed at the discomfort Marc showed at her frontal exposure! She called him a prude. Judy laughed again, and said she would leave before the big boy got in trouble!

Captain Marc Trembley, the tough soldier, the deadly CIA Agent and the supreme martial artist, was simply out of his depth with this beautiful woman! She just wasn't in any of his equations!

In the midst of his confusion Judy acted! In the twinkle of an eye she put her blouse on over the T-shirt. She then kissed Marc on the cheek, and left.

Marc laughed for a full minute after she left. He didn't know himself if the laugh was from being delighted, or relieved? He did know he was emotionally tired so he showered and went to bed. He even forgave any martial exercise or meditation for sleep.

The following day was a clear and warm Monday.

A cool and energetic Marc Trembley approached Dean Anders office with confidence, and with supreme composure of mind and body. He was satisfied that all would be well in his world.

Marc approached the Administration Building with a lightness of heart. Suddenly Josh Logan was blocking his path. The lightness seemed to get a little bit heavier when Marc noticed the two big bruisers moving quickly into strategic positions behind him.

Marc was not phased by all the adversaries, and he took the initiative. He advanced to Logan, and proceeded to shake his hand.

Josh Logan was amazed, and confused! He seemed to stand still in time.

Marc continued the initiative, but this time with conversation! "I'm sorry that we had differences in the past, but it was mostly my fault. I thought that next year football could find it's way into my schedule."

Unknown to the protagonists Dean Anders(who had seen the developments) moved close to the four men. He watched Josh Logan who was paralyzed into inaction.

Logan was dumfounded! He was thinking, "this s. o. b. had destroyed him on the football field, and was now shaking his hand!"

The two linebackers had no paralysis, they moved in for the kill.

Before they got to Marc, Dean Anders intercepted them. He grasped one mans left, 2nd one man's right wrist in a grip of steel.

"Gentlemen, you will be late for classes" Anders icy voice proclaimed!

"Disperse!"

The two men's faces displayed their amazement and surprise. They left for classes at a double time's pace!

Marc took the initiative again and patted Logan on the back. He exclaimed, "I'll see you at the tryouts!"

Marc and Anders left the confused Logan and headed toward the Deans office.

Logan heard the Dean say to Trembley "There may be hope for you yet, Marc Trembley!"

The new friends entered Anders office on a note of harmony and even comradeship.

Jane(the Dean's Secretary) was surprised, but pleased that the untidy older student and the meticulous Dean seemed to have become fast friends!

"Jane, I am not to be interrupted for the next hour." directed the Dean! No phones and no meetings! Understand?"

What followed was a two hour open ended conversation. Marc opened up to the Dean as he had never done before. He covered the military, CIA, and his personal life.

A receptive listener, it seemed that Dean Anders had a more than casual or perfunctory interest and knowledge of the intelligence community!

Dean Anders reticence at the moment appeared more formality than personal conviction.

Marc found out that Anders own background had a military contingent. He was from the Korean era more than the Vietnam era although his depth of knowledge on Vietnam seemed to be more than chance.

Anders had been a full "Bird" Colonel in Korea. Although nothing of his specialty was forth coming from this usually tight lipped man.

It was evident that he was ready to advise and even "tutor" this Captain Marc Trembley sitting opposite him. "But why, and to what extent?", was the question.

After the two hours, Marc and Anders parted as good friends, and even possible co-conspirators?

Anders had some insights into the intelligence community that were quite fascinating, even to tough veteran Marc Trembley.

Some of his contacts may have even crossed Robertson's or Robello's path.

Anders had the depth and extent of background knowledge that a CIA or ASA Bureau Chief would have at his fingertips. Interesting possibilities and probabilities loomed on the horizon.

"Was this University a CIA enclave, or was it just academia with a flush of patriotism?" Marc wondered! Probably he would never know. Or, would he?

Marc descended the Administration Building steps even as he had ascended them many moons ago.

The sky was bright and clear with the smell of fall in the air. This day had the ring of his first day, hopefully, the air of a new beginning. This feeling grasped his whole being. He was one with nature and man. In his mind nothing stirred, the air and land were still.

A slightly metallic sound became the only irritant to Marc's supreme tranquillity.

Marc turned quickly on the balls of his feet toward the offending sound.

The barrel of the standard issue nine millimeter revolver stared at him at him with dumb savagery that was oblivious to life or death. Staring down the other end of the barrel was Kim.

Then, from about fifty feet away come the sound of two simultaneous explosions, even as Marc started to shift his weight!

The next thing Marc heard was an oath and a scream. It was as if a bad dream was being played out, and Marc could do nothing about it! Then nothing, only blackness!

The blow was as clean and precise as a surgeons, but with just enough power to obliterate the light not the life. The superlative martial artist had been surpassed by a superior artist to save him and not to kill him! The blow to Marc's head had knocked him to the side enough to simultaneously get the expert shot off that impacted it's target! Marc's "control" had closed his dossier with deaths finality. His plan completed he left the scene.

A week had elapsed since the confusing episode when Kim had been killed. He still didn't quite know why, and by whom? He only knew that he had been assaulted from behind by the supreme ultimate assassin. But why had he been allowed to live? The blow had been delivered with blinding speed, but not with the power to kill! It was a chilling thought to mull over.

The air was dank with threatening storm clouds, and the new out grass stuck to the mans brightly polished shoes.

A short distance away a small group of mourners with umbrellas gathered around the open pit in the sodden ground. The umbrellas could not ward of the cold windy rain of the "Montreal Express."

A black hearse pulled up to the grave site with the accustomed precision of purpose that was it's duty.

No mindless machine this conveyance from Detroit.

Yet, the misery in death was overshadowed by the release from the strains of life the deceased had borne! His hard trek in life had led him almost inexplicably to this his final rest.

One of the mourners slipped a bandaged hand under his raincoat. With a little effort he laid the extracted green beret on the coffin. He made a Taoist bow, then returned to the ranks of the mourners again.

Captain Marc R. Trembley's slight smile was not a laugh at his fallen antagonist. It was a smile of relief that his own day of reckoning had not come! Not as yet.

A Little Tempered Metal

A little tempered metal garnered for the task
Awaiting only mindset, cast in mystic ages past

The body set in supple stone, potent cogent tool
Set to draw on inner self, extend from inner pool

All limbs rooted in the earth, support mobile action set
The C'hi sinks to his Tian Tiem, the inner self is ready yet

The mind is held aloft by concentrations string
The thread from root to limb, balanced
Yet light as the wind in spring

With rounded movement the deer springs
The tiger claws and the bird is on the wing

The Animal Frolics continue, with consummate power and grace
And the power of T'ai Chi Chuan resumes
Preceding time and space

William E. Dickinson
Poet and Author